FOREVER WITH THE FORBIDDEN

SUBMITTING TO MY STEPBROTHER
BOOK EIGHT

M. FRANCIS HASTINGS

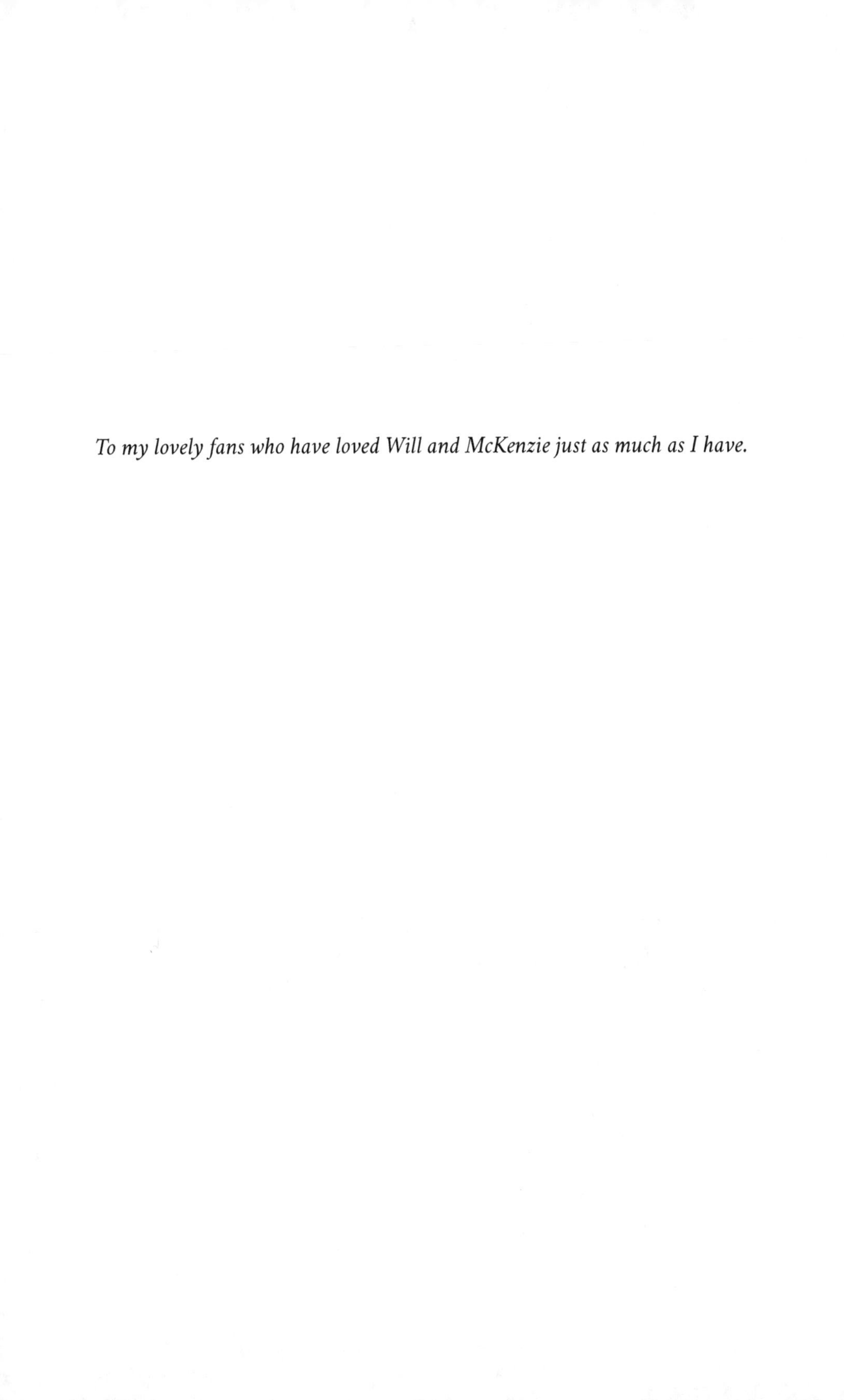

To my lovely fans who have loved Will and McKenzie just as much as I have.

CONTENTS

1

OUT COLD

WILL

"Ohhh, Will," McKenzie moaned, moving her hips with mine.

I kissed her, silencing her with my tongue.

Will!

I frowned. *That was weird.* I knew the voice wasn't McKenzie's. It was male.

Plus, I was kissing her, so she couldn't have said it herself.

It was more like a thought, actually, but it wasn't me, either.

Will!

I pulled back a little. "Do you hear something?"

She blinked up at me. "Seriously? You stopped? For wh—?"

"Will!" We both heard it clearly.

McKenzie pushed me off her and sat up abruptly. "It's Dad!"

I jumped off the bed, not even thinking about anything else. Then I did think. "Stay here. He's calling for me. Not you or your mom. Something must be wrong."

"I'm not going to—!"

I kissed her again. "Please." I didn't wait for an answer. I yanked on my boxers and ran down the hall.

Caleb and Jacey's door was closed, but I could hear a commotion inside. Then it stopped.

"... I'm sorry..." Moose said as I threw open the door.

Something about the situation was terribly wrong. Moose had a knee on Caleb's ravaged chest and was pressing a syringe into his neck.

"Will?" Moose looked at me, startled.

I didn't hesitate. I hit him with a flying tackle.

Moose grunted and fought back. He was ex-Special Forces, and I was an ex-football player. It wasn't really a contest, even with our age difference, but I had to do something.

He soon had me pinned with a knee on my throat. "You weren't supposed to see this, Will."

I couldn't answer, of course, and I had no idea what the *fuck* was going on, but I glared at him just the same.

"Now what am I goin' to do?" he muttered to himself. "I can't exactly turn you into a vegetable."

A vegetable? He'd been about to turn Caleb into a vegetable? Why?

"I'm tradin' you all for Dolly," he explained without my asking. "Caleb heard me talkin' to Shep. Shep don't approve but it's not like there's anythin' he can do about it. Shit. This is a problem."

"You're damn right it is."

I couldn't see, but I knew it was Jacey's voice.

"Moose, get off of Will before you suffocate him," she said coldly. "McKenzie, get that awful thing out of your father's neck. Is there anything left in it?"

He got off me, and I coughed. I turned to see Jacey in the doorway.

Holding a gun.

McKenzie raced past me and carefully pulled the syringe from her father's neck. "It's more than half full."

"What did you inject him with?" Jacey asked coldly.

Moose had his hands raised. I got to my feet, making sure not to get in the way of Jacey's crosshairs, and went over to Caleb, kneeling beside him.

Blood was pooling through his shirt. I wondered what sort of damage Moose had inflicted on his ravaged body.

"It's not somethin' you'd recognize," Moose said. "But I was just—"

"Just trying to turn my husband into a vegetable?" Jacey's voice was dangerously soft. It gave me chills all the way down my spine.

Even Moose understood his situation. "Ain't no one else here who can heal him back up. Look, he's bleedin'."

"It's cute you think I'd let you lay a finger on my husband now. Downright adorable," Jacey murmured. Her gun did not waver. "Will, please check Caleb's chest."

I ripped open Caleb's shirt while McKenzie hovered nearby. "It looks like it's a few pulled stitches, but I don't know what kind of damage might be inside. Moose was kneeling on his chest when I came in."

Jacey turned white with rage. "He was kneeling on his chest?"

"And trying to inject him with this," McKenzie added, holding up the syringe.

"I see." Jacey looked at Moose with a flame in her eyes I'd come to recognize.

It was vengeance.

"Now, Jacey, I want you to think about what you're plannin' to d —" Moose began.

Jacey pulled the trigger.

Moose dropped to the floor with a hole in his head.

"Thought about it, thanks," she seethed. Then she looked at the gun as though it was the most disgusting thing she'd ever touched, and tossed it on the bed.

"What do we do, Mom?" McKenzie asked.

Jacey batted us out of the way and knelt next to her husband. She took his hand. "Caleb? Caleb, my love? Please wake up."

McKenzie and I stood helplessly by while Jacey tried over and over again to bring him around. None of us even bothered with the dead man on the floor.

I noticed McKenzie was still holding the syringe. I plucked it from her fingers and put it on the bedside table.

"Will," Jacey finally said to me, her voice raspy with tears. "I need you to find Moose's burner phone. I know he must have one."

"Right." I started in the first place I could think of. I began patting down Moose's body, ignoring the blood and brain matter.

"Who are we calling, Mom?" McKenzie asked as I pulled the phone out triumphantly from the back pocket of Moose's jeans.

"Nine-one-one," Jacey replied. "We have no choice. Moose is dead and none of us knows how to fix this."

McKenzie's shoulders drooped. "Okay. I understand. Hopefully Ike won't be too mad—"

I double-clicked a side button to get the emergency option. All I had to do was press the icon. "It'll be okay, honeybee. We'll figure it out."

"Will, give me the phone," Jacey said calmly.

"I've got it. I'm just about to—"

"Don't do anything. Just give me the phone," she repeated.

I frowned in confusion, but handed Jacey the phone. "I don't understand."

"Will, I need you to take McKenzie, and Moose's truck, and get out of here." Jacey's tone was still measured and calm. "Shep, Caleb, and I will stay."

"Mom, no!" McKenzie knelt on the floor next to her mother, hugging her tightly. "No. We'll all go together. We're family, we—"

Jacey leaned her cheek on McKenzie's shoulder. "Honey, your father and I could never live with ourselves if we knew we'd caused you to be trapped like we were. It hurts my soul to know what you've endured already. I can't say Masterson's goons won't catch up to you. But I have to give you a fighting chance. You're my daughter. And, had circumstances been different, Will would have been my son. I can't let you two get captured. I can't."

I swallowed hard as McKenzie began to cry. "We'll figure it out, honeybee. We'll get them back."

"You will do nothing of the sort!" Jacey said sharply. "You are *not* getting involved anymore. Do you hear me, Will Masterson?"

"I know there are things we can do," I argued.

Jacey brought her head up and fixed me with a look I imagined mothers everywhere used to shrink a misbehaving child down to the size of a peanut. "You will do nothing but get McKenzie out of here and as far from Masterson's circle as you can. That is what you are going to do."

"Mom, I'm sure—" McKenzie tried.

"*You will do as I say!*" Jacey shouted.

My hackles went up. I was a thirty-year-old man, for God's sake. She wasn't going to stop me from trying to save them. "Listen to me —"

Caleb groaned. "Will?"

We stopped fighting and turned to look at him.

I scrambled over and put my face where he could see me without straining himself. "Yes, Caleb? I'm here."

"You came." He smiled tiredly. "Didn't know if you would."

"Of course I did. McKenzie got the syringe out of your neck before he got much in you. I hope there's no permanent damage," I said.

He blinked a few times. "I just feel tired. Not brain dead. Wait, McKenzie came, too?!"

"And Jacey. She shot Moose. He's dead," I explained.

Caleb relaxed. "That's good. Jacey? Baby, are you okay?"

Jacey burst into tears and snuggled into his side. "What do you mean, 'am I okay'? Are *you* okay?"

"I think so. Chest hurts." He winced.

"Yes, I'm calling an ambulance as soon as these stubborn kids get out of here," Jacey said. "I'm trying to make them promise not to try to rescue us later, but they are so bull-headed!"

He nodded. "McKenzie, Will, do as she says."

"We have options!" I responded, exasperated.

"No. You don't. Now, please leave before I bleed out," he whispered.

"And don't come back." Jacey's voice shook, but she was adamant nonetheless.

I decided not to argue any further. I wasn't going to make any promises, but I also wasn't going to wait any longer. Caleb needed help, and I needed to take care of McKenzie. "I'll find Moose's keys."

"That's not a promise," Jacey pointed out.

"It's the best I can do," I said and began feeling around Moose's pockets again. I found his keys in his right pocket. Standing, I held my hand out to McKenzie. "We need to go."

She hesitated, staring at her parents. "I don't want them to get hurt."

"Your mom isn't going to call nine-one-one until we leave. Your dad's already hurt. We need to go," I replied softly.

McKenzie bit her quivering lower lip, then hugged Jacey. "I love you, Mom."

"I love you, too, sweetheart," Jacey whispered back.

"What am I, chopped liver?" Caleb chuckled, then groaned.

"Dad! Don't hurt yourself!" She kissed him carefully on the forehead. "Take care of yourself. And Mom."

"Always do." He teared up a little bit. "Now, you go with Will. Go."

McKenzie choked back a sob then grabbed my hand.

I pulled her to her feet and wrapped her in my arms. "We're going to be okay. Now let's get out of here so they can call an ambulance."

She nodded.

I tugged her out into the hall.

"Is he dead?" Shep called from his bedroom.

I froze. "Um... yes, Shep. I'm sorry."

Shep was quiet for a moment. "They callin' an ambulance for us?"

"Yes. But McKenzie and I are leaving first. If you think you can make it, you're welcome to come," I said.

"No. You go. We need medical attention. Good luck to you," he replied.

"Thank you. Good luck to you, too." I maneuvered McKenzie into our room to get proper clothes on, then out of the cabin.

The truck was still parked in the tall grass, red and rusty as ever. I opened the driver's door, then unlocked the passenger side.

McKenzie slipped into the truck, looking devastated.

I was sure she was.

Once I was inside, I put the key int0 the ignition and turned it.

There was a click, but the engine didn't turn over.

"What the…?" I tried again.

This time, there wasn't even a click.

"Will?" she asked. "What's wrong?"

I puzzled over the situation. "I don't know."

The radio came on then. Or at least the screen did. It was displaying a countdown from sixty.

"Oh my God he rigged the truck to blow!" she gasped.

"Get out of the truck!" I shouted at her.

She was just staring at the screen.

"GET OUT OF THE TRUCK!!!" I yelled, kicking my door open. I grabbed her arm and pulled, but she'd already put her seat belt on. "MCKENZIE!!!"

McKenzie shook herself and undid her seat belt. She jumped across the cab and landed in my arms.

We both tumbled to the ground. I sprang to my feet and hauled McKenzie up with me, running for the trees. Once inside the tree line, I pushed McKenzie to the ground and laid over her.

There wasn't a second to spare. The truck exploded.

The trees took the worst of the shrapnel. I felt a few scratches on my back, but nothing like Caleb had endured. Still, I would have endured it, just like him. For McKenzie, I would have happily endured anything.

She shook me off and sat up. Then she began patting me down. "Will, are you okay?"

I took her hands in mine. "I'm fine. Are you okay?"

McKenzie nodded. "Thanks to you."

There was a scream from the cabin. "MCKENZIE!!! WILL!!!"

It was Jacey.

"We should go back and tell Mom we're okay," McKenzie sighed.

I paused, then shook my head. "No."

"No?" she responded, confused.

"If they think we're dead, then we might have a better chance of getting them out. Because if they think we're dead, Ike might think we're dead, and he won't be expecting us," I said.

She bit her lip. "But… they're going to be so broken over it."

"It's the only advantage we have right now. We can at least give it a try." I shrugged.

McKenzie mulled it over. Then she gave in with a sigh. "Okay."

"Okay?" I asked.

"Okay," she confirmed.

"Now we just need to figure out how to get the *fuck* out of here without getting caught," I said, sitting up and looking around.

She pointed toward the lake. "Rowboat."

I followed her finger. There was, indeed, an old wooden rowboat sitting on the shore.

"Perfect."

2
ROW, ROW, ROW

McKenzie

I felt awful as we scrabbled down the soft incline. Mom and Dad were going to lose their minds! My stomach was all tied up in knots. But Will did have a point—if we wanted to save them in the long run, we needed to be dead for now.

The boat was heavy, but between Will and I, we got it in the water. He held it steady by the bow. "Hop in."

"You're going to shove us off?" I asked.

He nodded. "I think I have a stronger kick. This thing is a beast. We're going to have to make sure it clears the sand."

"True." I climbed into the boat and sat in the middle seat. The bottom was already puddling with water. I hoped this wasn't a bad sign.

It wasn't as though we had other options.

Will kicked the boat away from the shore, jumping in at the last second. We felt the bow bump the sandy bottom. I held my breath.

Luckily, it was just that one bump, and then we were just floating on water.

"This can't be good," he said, noting the same water slowly pooling in the bottom of the boat that I had.

"Should we get out and swim?" I asked, somewhat sarcastically. Then I hung my head. "Sorry. I just feel like crap."

"And I'm the one who said we can't tell your parents we're alive. I get it," he said, gently patting my knee. "We should get ourselves out of sight. There are some trees hanging over the water over there. Let's see if we can't camp out there until the cavalry leaves."

"Okay, sounds good." I reached for an oar.

He stopped me. "Let's see if I can do it myself. We can't both get tired at the same time."

I frowned at him suspiciously. "That had better be the reason. Don't go all toxic masculinity on me now, Will Masterson the Third."

"I'm not going all 'toxic masculinity'!" he scoffed. He grabbed the oars and started to row.

I eyed him askance as we cut quickly through the water. I couldn't argue with his strength and speed. If I'd taken the other oar, would I have been able to keep up? Or would we have turned in comical little circles, bickering in the middle of the lake?

The image made me laugh a little.

"What?" he asked.

"I was just thinking about each of us taking an oar and how you're stronger than me, so we'd end up spinning in circles, arguing with each other," I admitted.

He chuckled. "Yes, I think that's how we would have ended up."

"I really am sorry for snarking at you," I said contritely.

"I know."

We fell silent as sirens sounded behind us. I turned to look and saw emergency vehicles pulling up to Moose's little cabin.

"Will they see us?" I asked worriedly.

"We're almost there." Sure enough, we slid under the overhanging branches of the leaning trees not five minutes later.

I grabbed one branch to hold the boat in place and he grabbed another. We bobbed on the gentle waves rolling toward the shore.

We could just barely see three stretchers come out of the house. I held my breath as each emerged, then let it out as I noted only one of them was completely covered with a sheet. Dad, and Shep, were still alive.

Mom stumbled out of the house after them. One of the emergency personnel—I couldn't tell if it was a police officer or someone else—caught her and motored her along.

"This is going to kill her," I whispered, my throat choking up with tears.

"She'll forgive us. We have to get them out, and the only advantage I can think of is if Ike thinks we're dead," he reminded me.

I sighed. "I know."

The firefighters were out toward the road, busy putting out the truck fire. The smoke and mist of water in the air blocked our view of the grassy driveway, so we didn't see the black town car approaching until it was right on top of the ambulance.

I stiffened. "Will?"

The doors of the sedan opened and four men, three quite burly, stepped out.

"I have a bad feeling," he replied.

The three burly men approached the person who had Mom by the arm. They started talking.

Then, all of a sudden, the one holding Mom transferred her over to the big, burly men.

"Oh no!" I gasped.

"Shit." Will touched my shoulder.

The smaller man, meanwhile, had gone over to who I assumed was the fire chief. They spoke for a while, the fire chief gesturing at the scattered debris. The smaller man nodded, then took out his phone.

"Is Mom going to be okay?" I asked worriedly.

"I don't know," Will admitted. "I do know Ike is about to start a full-on search for us. If they can't figure out whether or not we were in the bombing, Ike's going to do a thorough search just in case." He was clearly stressed. "We can't move until they're gone, but if Ike brings in more people, they'll find us for sure if we stay here."

I'd wanted to focus more on my parents' situation, but he was clearly more preoccupied with ours. I looked around and noted a couple of big rocks sticking out of the water near the shore. "We can get out here and make our way to the next cabin. Maybe we can borrow their car?"

"We'd be stealing that car. And, hopefully, we can," he said. "But we can't go rowing out where they can see us—"

"The rocks," I responded, pointing. "We can get to shore here."

He looked. "But the boat...."

"It'll be empty. It might look a little suspicious, but it's not like we'll be in it," I said.

Will thought for a moment, then sighed. "There's nothing for it. You're right, that's our best option."

Together, we used the branches to maneuver the boat as close to the rocks as we could. Then, he held a branch and I crawled out of the boat and onto the nearest rock, standing unsteadily.

"This is going to be the hard part," he said. "You're going to have to get to the next rock and try to hold onto the boat at the same time."

I looked at the next rock and gulped. It was going to be quite a stretch!

Still, I moved to the next rock, trying to keep my tennis shoes from sliding. Once I righted myself, I reached for the boat...

... And almost tumbled into the water.

"McKenzie!" he cried, stumbling across the boat as though there was something he could do.

"Don't move!" I replied, reaching out for the boat and grabbing the side just before it would have floated out of reach.

He stopped floundering around and waited for me to get into a better position.

I was still pretty precarious by the time I found a way to stand that kept me out of the water. But I wasn't going to tell him that. "Okay. Get to that rock."

Will slowly got out of the boat.

As soon as he let go of the branches and the boat was free to squirm around, I slipped and started to fall.

Strong arms grabbed me around the waist and held me up. "Let go of the boat," Will said.

I was more than happy to. As it drifted off, I stood in his arms, panting.

"Well, we could have done that more gracefully," he muttered.

"We'll do it better next time," I teased.

He groaned and kissed the back of my neck. "Please tell me there won't be a next time."

"You never know with us." I looked behind me and saw he had one foot on my rock and one foot on his. "Do you think if you let go of me so I can get to shore, you'll fall in?"

"Don't worry. I think I've got pretty good balance," he said. He slowly let me go.

I wanted to kiss him, or ruffle his hair, or something. But I also didn't want to tip him into the lake. "Let me know if you need help," I replied worriedly instead. I began using the rough, wet rocks like stepping stones to get to the shore.

To my relief, he was right behind me. I grabbed a bent tree trunk to haul myself over the low beach and up onto the grass. Then, I got out of the way so Will could do the same.

We sat in the grass catching our breaths for a moment.

Then, he took my hand and stood, pulling me to my feet. "We need to find a car to steal."

"Okay." We started up the grassy hill that led to the cabin above us. Like Moose's cabin, it was small. Unlike Moose's cabin….

"I think it might be empty," I said, noting the drawn drapes and dusty outdoor furniture.

"I suppose we'll have to go to the next one for a vehicle, then," he sighed. We started up the overgrown driveway.

Then, I saw it.

"Will!" I pulled him to a stop. "Look!"

There was a small patch off the driveway that had something covered on it. It was about the size of a truck.

"Yes!" He kissed me. "You are an *angel*!"

"You remember that the next time we have a fight," I grinned.

He walked over to the canvas and pulled it off with a flourish. It was, indeed, an old green truck with a tonneau cover.

"Start looking for the keys." He went to the cab of the truck.

I began feeling around the wheel wells. Then I opened the fuel door and the keys tumbled to the ground. I snatched them up and waved them triumphantly at Will.

"Honeybee, you are not just an angel, you are a *miracle*," he said.

"I suppose you think you're driving?" I responded, raising an eyebrow at him.

Will and I did a little dance around each other, but he finally used his height to pluck the keys out of my hand. "You can chalk it up to toxic masculinity," he chuckled.

I punched him lightly in the arm. "I'll get you back for this, Will Masterson the Third."

"Is that a promise?" He used his sexy voice.

"Maybe," I said flippantly. I got in the passenger side without further argument.

We closed the doors and just stared at the dashboard for a moment. Will's hand hovered near the ignition, the keys dangling from his fingertips.

"It's… really unlikely it would happen twice." I laughed nervously.

"It also wouldn't surprise me if Moose owns every cabin on this pond," he murmured.

We swallowed at the same time.

Then Will leaned over and kissed me hard.

"I love you," he said.

Then he shoved the key in the ignition and turned it.

3

ON OUR OWN

WILL

We didn't explode.

The engine didn't turn over right away, but we didn't explode.

The truck not starting was definitely to be expected—who knew how long it had sat idle out in the wilderness?

When the engine finally turned over, we both let out a sigh of relief. I gave McKenzie a weak smile. She gave me one back.

"I guess the universe is looking out for us a little bit," I said.

She frowned and socked me in the arm.

"Ow! What?" I asked, rubbing the spot.

"Don't say that! It's like… begging something bad to happen! Oh my God, is there any wood in here to knock on?" She searched around frantically.

I put a hand on her knee. "It's fine. We're fine. Let's just go."

McKenzie scowled at me while I put the car in gear, but then did, grudgingly, take my hand.

I held hands with her as I maneuvered the truck out of the woods and onto the gravel road. I knew which direction Moose's cabin was. I decided to go the opposite way and hope the road had some sort of outlet to a highway on the other side.

We curved around the lake and I started to worry that we were going to end up head-on with Ike and his people. But then, mercifully, the road twisted away from the small lake and meandered over to a larger one.

"Where are we?" she asked once we came out onto a blacktopped road.

"Somewhere near Grand Marais, I believe. Didn't you say your parents spent some time there?" I replied.

"Yeah, they said they liked it a lot. Maybe we should stay there until we—" She groaned.

"What?" I asked, worried she might be injured.

She gave me a despairing look. "We don't have any money."

My breath stopped. "We don't..."

"... Have any money," she finished for me.

I glanced down at the different dials on the old truck's dashboard. Half a tank of gas.

Would it be enough to get us anywhere?

"How are we going to figure this out?" she asked.

"I...." I wanted to say something brave. Something reassuring. But we were past lying to each other. "I don't know."

McKenzie sat for a moment, then began rummaging through the glove compartment.

"What are you doing?" I asked.

"I'm looking for anything we can sell," she said. "Maybe the title of the truck?"

"Good thinking. Is there a map in there?" I pulled over to the side of the road and took papers as she handed them to me.

The insurance card, which was expired, said the truck belonged to Leonard Hawkins. I was willing to bet the tags were expired as well.

We were pull-me-over bait, which only made our situation worse.

And there was no title to be found.

"Maybe there will be something in the back," I said, opening my door and stepping out of the truck. I unlatched the tonneau cover and dropped the tailgate.

McKenzie came up behind me.

I just stared for a moment, then crawled into the back. Four red, plastic gas cans sat snugly next to each other. I gave each one a shake, finding them full. "Well," I said with a laugh. "We've got gas. How are the truck's tags?"

She lifted the tailgate a bit to check. "They'll be good for another month."

I sagged with relief. "Good. That's good."

"But neither of us is carrying a driver's license," she sighed. "Or money. I mean, we can sleep in the truck, but what are we going to eat? And what if we get pulled over?"

My stomach took that opportunity to grumble.

"See? Mine's doing that, too." She sat down on the tailgate and wrapped her arms around herself.

I moved up behind her and wrapped my arms around her as well. I dropped my chin on her shoulder. "We'll figure something out because we have to."

"I wish there was someone we could call. Someone who'd help." She leaned into me.

"We'll—"

"Oh!" McKenzie's head came up and she nearly knocked me in the chin. "I could call Gwendolyn!"

"Gwendolyn?" I echoed, doubtful.

She nodded. "I think she's a good person. She might be able to spare a couple hundred until we can figure things out. We'd pay her back, of course."

"Of course," I agreed. "But... honeybee... she's dating Bran."

"All the more reason to contact her. I think she feels bad about what happened at his house. She might really want to help us," she said.

I grimaced. "I don't know...."

"I do. I mean, we can at least try, right?" She gave me an intense look.

Of all our options, it really wasn't the most horrible. And, as she said, we could at least ask. "All right. I'll get us to a gas station, and we can see if we can use their phone."

McKenzie smiled and kissed me, then trotted back to the passenger seat.

I sighed and shook my head, doing up the tailgate and tonneau cover before getting back behind the wheel.

We drove another hour before a tiny gas station came into view. I parked in one of the two parking spots available.

She jumped out of the truck as soon as it stopped and raced to the door. I figured she needed to use the restroom, but she went straight to the counter. "Excuse me, sir," she was saying by the time I got inside. "I was wondering if we could use your phone. Ours were stolen."

It wasn't a lie. They had been stolen—a while ago.

"Sure, gorgeous." The attendant gave her a smile I didn't like and handed over the store phone.

I walked up behind her, intent on asserting myself, but she swatted me away. I frowned.

The attendant laughed. "Trouble in paradise."

McKenzie ignored us both. "Hello, Gwendolyn?"

I was shocked she remembered her number off the top of her head!

"Yeah, hi, it's McKenzie. No, no, don't apologize. It wasn't your fault at all. Listen, Will and I are in a bit of trouble. We're stranded out near Grand Marais, and we don't have money or phones. We do have a truck and gas but… that's it. I was wondering if we could borrow some money," she said.

The attendant raised an eyebrow. "Dang, they totally fleeced you, huh?"

"They did," I confirmed. Also, not a lie. I'd been stripped of my own financial autonomy.

"I know Will'ssituation,n and I know it's hard to believe but… listen, you can't tell anybody. Especially anybody connected with Will," she continued. "It's extremely important. I mean it. Life or death."

I held my breath, wondering what the reaction to those words would be. McKenzie was as tense as a piano wire.

Then she relaxed. "Thanks, Gwendolyn."

I let my breath out slowly, relieved.

"Yeah, we can meet you in Grand Marais. Where?" she asked.

There was a pause, and I raised an eyebrow.

"She's looking," McKenzie mouthed.

"The Angry Trout Cafe," the attendant suggested.

Something helpful from the peanut gallery. I nodded. "That sounds good."

"The Angry Trout Cafe?" she said into the phone. "Okay, yeah. We'll meet you there. In… five hours, you say?"

That would take us to a late dinner, but I wasn't about to look a gift horse in the mouth. Plus, it took at least four-and-a-half hours to get to Grand Marais from Minnetonka.

"We'll be there. Thank you, Gwendolyn. You have no idea how much this means to us," she murmured.

McKenzie was tearing up a bit, so I put an arm around her.

"Aw, paradise restored," the attendant grinned. "But you didn't have to go to all that trouble just for me. I would have let you use the phone anyway."

She blushed as she handed the phone back to the attendant. "Thank you."

"No problem. And good luck," the attendant said.

"Thank you," we replied together.

He took out a handful of granola bars and two big bottles of water. "This should hold you over. Oh, and I won't tell Dan you stole his truck. Just make sure you leave it somewhere the cops can find it."

Now it was both our turns to be embarrassed. "Sorry," I mumbled. "We were in a bit of a bind."

"Everybody's running from something," the attendant said sagely.

We took the bars and the water.

Then McKenzie suddenly leaned over the counter and kissed him on the cheek. "You are a truly wonderful person."

He smiled. "Thanks."

I felt a little jealous, but also so grateful that I could hardly object.

The phone rang.

"Is it Gwendolyn?" she asked.

The attendant answered quickly. "Hello?" He frowned, then his eyebrows shot up as he looked at us.

My muscles tensed to run.

"Nah, I don't know who was calling that number. I left the phone in the back," he lied easily. "But yeah, that sure is a lot of money, sir. The gas station cameras? They aren't hooked up really well. We hardly get any footage, and even then, it's grainy." He crossed to a computer that showed three inside views of the gas station and one outside. I saw him erase the last four hours of footage, then turn the whole thing off altogether. "Yeah, real bummer I can't help you out. Sure, you're welcome to drop by." He waved at us to leave. "See you soon."

McKenzie and I all but ran out of the gas station. Our seatbelts weren't even properly fastened when I peeled out of our parking spot.

I rolled the window down and waved.

He gave us a thumbs-up. But then, he picked up the phone again.

I had a bad feeling.

"It's a gas station," McKenzie said as though reading my thoughts. "He probably had to answer another call."

"I hope so," I mumbled.

GRAND MARAIS WAS A BEAUTIFUL SEASIDE TOWN WITH ITS OWN lighthouse. The shoreline was dotted with rough rock and boats. Set back just a bit were restaurants and hotels.

With nothing better to do, I parked the truck on an out-of-the-way street and McKenzie and I took a nap, relying on the dashboard clock to tell us when five hours had elapsed.

At four-and-a-half hours, I was just about to drive us to The Angry Trout Cafe, when there was a knock at the back window.

We both jumped.

I began rehearsing an excuse in my head to tell the officer—I was sure it was a cop—when they got to my window.

Instead, Gwendolyn popped into view.

I rolled down my window. "Gwendolyn? I thought we were meeting you at the Angry Trout?"

"The guy on the phone said I needed to ditch my phone and *not* go to the Angry Trout. He was afraid our conversation was recorded," she said.

The guy… the attendant!

I could have kissed the man myself in that moment.

Then another head appeared and my stomach clenched. "Tracy?!"

"Don't get your undies in a twist. I'm the money," Tracy said while McKenzie leaned over my shoulder.

"Tracy Franz…" McKenzie whispered tensely.

I swallowed. I was well aware.

This was Morgan Franz's daughter. Morgan Franz, one of my grandfather's associates in that illegal cabal I was supposed to join.

"Does… your father know you're here, Tracy?" I put my hand over McKenzie's as it rested on my shoulder.

"That would kind of defeat the purpose, don't you think?" Tracy waved a hand. "He'd tell Ike, and then Ike would make you go home— I don't know why you missed your grandfather's funeral, but I figure there must be a good reason. Gwendolyn told me what Bran did. That asshole. Anyway, I decided, whatever this is, I'm going to help."

"Why?" McKenzie and I asked together.

Tracy snorted. "Because sometimes you just have to do the right thing. And because Gwendolyn asked, and I owe her. Father was trying to set up some kind of arranged marriage with Bran. She told me about his true colors. I told Father I wouldn't do it. He was *pissed*, but it's not like he can force me down the aisle and make me say the words."

"Oh God! Do *not* marry that man!" McKenzie gasped.

"Like I said, I'm not going to. So, how much do you need?" Tracy asked.

"Maybe a couple hundred," McKenzie suggested.

I didn't have the heart to tell her that wouldn't get us very far. "Um… maybe a little more."

Tracy rolled her eyes. "It's adorable that you're trying to be so modest, but you're on the run from Ike Freeborn. The man's a bloodhound. I mean, he's brought you back like three or four times? I'm just guessing. It's like you show up, then disappear, then show up again. I don't know what you're running from, but you've got to be more realistic." She opened my door and shoved a carry-on suitcase into my arms. "Here. There's a hundred-thousand in there. I got it from Father's safe before we left. I think you can make it work."

I was speechless.

McKenzie was not. "Oh my God, Tracy!"

"You're welcome." Tracy looked pointedly at me.

"Th-thank you," I stuttered.

"Good. Now we can all go to the hotel and you can tell me *all* about what the *fuck* is going on and what it has to do with my father," Tracy said. "I paid for it in cash, so they can't track our location."

"A-all right," I reluctantly agreed. I pushed the suitcase to McKenzie and hopped out of the truck so Gwendolyn and Tracy could get in behind us in the cab.

"East Bay Suites," Tracy requested. "It's down the road and to the left. I'd put it in my phone, but *somebody* said I had to leave that at home."

"You'll find out why in a minute," I mumbled, navigating us to the hotel.

"I hope so," Tracy replied.

4

TROUBLE FOR FOUR

McKenzie

The view of Lake Superior was spectacular from the three-bedroom suite. It had its own kitchen (which Tracy had stocked), a large sitting area, a beautiful gas fireplace surrounded by stone, and cute furnishings.

We settled in the sitting area; Will and I on the sofa, Gwendolyn and Tracy each in a chair.

"Talk," Tracy said as soon as our butts hit the cushions.

"What do you know about your father's work?" Will asked, taking my hand.

I threaded my fingers through his.

"He's a businessman," Tracy responded with a shrug. "A developer of some kind. Construction and stuff on a large scale. At least, that's what I've managed to pick up. He thinks I'm kind of a flake and says my job is to look pretty and marry well." Her 'carefree' laugh was a little bitter. "He very magnanimously allowed me to get a bachelor's degree in literature. He said it was trivial enough not to intimidate a good husband. I'd like to get a master's, but he said no."

"That... sucks..." I said sympathetically. "I mean, both that he views you that way and that he looks down on your major."

Tracy smiled slightly. "Thanks. I'll bet Will would want you to study whatever you want to. But Ike is an asshole. I've heard him arguing with my father in my father's office. Mostly Ike telling him to stay in his lane and do what he's told."

"Yeah, Ike and Masterson—er—Mr. Masterson, had it all planned out for me. They wanted me to go into International Affairs and help Will with that," I replied.

"Lucky," Tracy sighed. "I'd have liked that." Then she squared her shoulders. "So, Will, what's all this fuss about?"

He grimaced. "It's not going to be pretty."

"I figured not." Tracy crossed her arms over her chest. "Out with it."

"A lot of our families are in this kind of illegal acts ring, profiting off of human trafficking, illegal weapons sales, drugs, etc., etc. Just about anything you can think of that's dirty and awful, they have a hand in. My grandfather was the head, but now I think it's Ike. Your father's involved," he said. "I'm… very sorry. It was a shock to me, too."

Tracy nodded slowly. "I'm not really all that shocked. I'm disappointed in my father, but I'm not surprised. It explains all the secret meetings."

"I'm glad you're taking it so well." I tried to be encouraging.

"It's… a lot. But you explained it well." She looked at Gwendolyn. "I suppose Bran's in on it?"

"I don't know," Gwendolyn replied. "But it wouldn't surprise me."

"He is. But he's in the doghouse for trying to assault McKenzie and for being an idiot in the business in general," Will said.

Tracy laughed. "That makes even more sense. Though, sorry to hear Bran tried to assault you, McKenzie."

"He beat me up a bit. But then Ike hired someone to throw acid on him so… I think he's been punished," I responded.

"It's nice to know Ike isn't just a little weasel." Tracy sat back in her chair and tapped her chin.

Gwendolyn touched her arm. "What are you going to do?"

"What I have to, of course. I'll have to go back and pretend like we just had a fun girls' weekend," Tracy said. "I can't run off with these two. Then everyone will get suspicious."

"What about the hundred-thousand dollars? Isn't your father going to blow a gasket?" Will asked.

"I've done it before. I'll just say my villa in the south of France needed immediate repairs, and I didn't have the money in my allowance. He keeps changing the safe code, but he can't remember anything with a number involved, so it's always something I already know. One of his and my stepmothers' wedding dates. His social security number. A registration for one of the yachts. Anything he can easily look up. Or he tapes the password under his desk. Idiot." Tracy shook her head. "I take it you keep running because they want you knee deep in their illegal activities."

"Yes," Will admitted. "And because McKenzie and her family are basically hostages because they found out and the Feds want them to testify against... well, my grandfather, but probably now against Ike and everyone else."

Tracy's features clouded with concern. "Wasn't your mother supposed to be at your engagement party?"

My stomach turned. "She was. But my dad is in a bad way, and they told her she could visit him. What they really wanted to do was make another Will. She was his surrogate."

"Oh my God!" Gwendolyn cried. "How horrific!"

"It failed but... I don't know what they'll do now," I said softly. "We kind of faked our own deaths."

"I don't know how long that will last," Will added. "Hopefully long enough to get the family out. Element of surprise and all that."

"Well, they're not going to hear anything from me," Tracy stated.

"Or me," Gwendolyn agreed.

I rubbed my thumb nervously over the back of his hand. "They're going to offer you a *lot* of money to tell you anything you know about us. I mean... life-changing money. I just want you to know now that I won't ever blame you if you decide to take it."

"I don't need money," Tracy responded. She turned to Gwendolyn.

"And if you ever need money, you just ask me. That's what best friends are for."

"Thanks," Gwendolyn said. "But I wouldn't take Freeborn's money. I'd always know where it came from and what it did to my friends. I don't want to live with that kind of guilt."

"You guys might be in danger now. If Ike even believes a little bit that you know what's going on…" Will warned.

"Ike can pound sand. He doesn't have the same power over me that he has over you. I doubt he'd put even a quarter of the resources he's put toward finding you into badgering me," Tracy scoffed.

I made a little noise of disagreement. "Something in Masterson's will, or in the contract they have, or both, says Ike needs Will in order to keep getting his hefty salary, and he can't run the company without him. So, he's going to do everything in his power to get Will back. He'll mow over anyone who gets in his way."

"Hm. Well, sounds like I need to go oversee the renovations to my villa in France," Tracy mused.

"Probably a good plan," he agreed.

"I might just go with you," Gwendolyn said to Tracy. "It seems the dating pool is getting too hot to handle on the circuit."

"We'll make a girls' month of it. Or year." Tracy looked at Will and me. "Have you figured out how you're going to get McKenzie's family back?"

"And two friends," he said.

"We don't really know," I mumbled.

Tracy looked thoughtful. "Well, if there's anything I can do on my end, I'll do it. We just need a way to contact each other that Ike can't hack."

"You're going to the south of France," he reminded her. "Kind of hard to send a carrier pigeon that far."

"Good point." She looked at Gwendolyn. "Maybe we'll stay."

"Stay? But that puts you in danger!" I protested. "Especially Gwendolyn."

"No, I'll stay, too," Gwendolyn decided. "These people are doing terrible things, and they're holding your family hostage. It isn't right."

"You need to understand," Will said very seriously. "Once you're in this, you never get out. Never."

"Ask my parents," I added.

"I will. Once they're out and the FBI has shut this business down. It's the only way out I see for you, really. For any of us," Tracy replied.

"But you're not in it yet. You don't have to be. You can live your life—" he tried.

"I'm in," Tracy said firmly.

"Me, too," Gwendolyn chimed in. "I mean, how often does the whore get to be the hero?"

"You're not a whore!" the other three of us insisted together.

Gwendolyn shrugged. "I am. But that puts me in a unique position to gather information. You'd be surprised how easily men let their guard down."

"I wouldn't be surprised at all," Tracy sniffed. "And I can look through my father's files. He'll have even worse passwords on his computer than on the safe, I'm sure. Or he'll have them taped under the desk. And he looks down on me for *my* intelligence."

"That just goes to show how much of a moron he is," Will said.

"So, how will we communicate?" Tracy asked.

I guessed there was no going back. "Burner phones?" I suggested.

Gwendolyn clapped her hands. "Excellent idea!"

"Great! Let's go get four." Tracy stood, and so did Gwendolyn.

"All right." Will gave in with a sigh and rose, holding his hand out to me.

"They don't understand what they're getting into," I whispered to him, worried.

"No," Will agreed, "they don't."

HALF AN HOUR LATER, ALL FOUR OF US HAD BURNER PHONES. TRACY and Gwendolyn were excited, as though they'd just become lead actors in a spy movie.

I felt terrible for them.

Will didn't look much better, a grumpy expression on his face. "You two can still—"

"Will. We're doing this. End of story. You two concentrate on staying under the radar. We'll keep our eyes and ears out for an opportunity," Tracy said. "The hotel room is paid for a week. Cash. You can stay there or take the money I gave you and go somewhere else, if you think it'd be safer. We'll stay in touch through the burner phones. Got it?"

"Got it." He sounded miserable.

"Good. I'd say let's go get you a car, but I don't think you have your IDs." Tracy puzzled over this. "I wish I knew someone who made fake IDs."

Gwendolyn coughed.

We all looked at her. "You know someone who does fake IDs?"

"Yes. He's not cheap, but they're flawless," she said.

"Where is he?" Tracy asked.

"Back in the cities. But don't worry. He can do it remotely," Gwendolyn replied. "He'll send the finished IDs to the hotel."

"Then we're getting you a laptop. And some clothes," Tracy decided.

"Tracy, you've already done so much," Will said.

"And I'm going to do a little more. Deal with it," Tracy responded.

5

A NEW IDENTITY

Will

"Alex Clay," I said, looking at myself in the hotel bathroom mirror. "Alex Clay."

"Naomi Johnson," McKenzie recited next to me. "Naomi Johnson."

We both held a passport and driver's license. Gwendolyn was right. As far as I could tell, they were flawless.

And, thanks to Tracy, they were overnighted to the hotel's front desk. She'd made a pit stop in Minneapolis before I'd even reached out to Gwendolyn's contact. I wasn't sure how much she'd paid him, but he was an extremely helpful, happy man.

"We should go buy a car," I told McKenzie once we'd rehearsed so much I'd almost forgotten I was anyone but Alex Clay.

"Yeah," she said. "What are we going to do with Dan's truck?"

"Oh. I parked it around the corner while you were napping and called in an anonymous tip to the police," I explained. "As far as I know, it's been towed."

"Did you wipe it down for fingerprints?" she asked anxiously.

I nodded. "I did. Don't worry, honeybee. We won't be easy to catch."

She relaxed and leaned against me. "I guess we're walking."

"We're calling a cab." We both had cell phones now, after all.

McKenzie hefted a large purse over her shoulder. It was where some of our money was. The rest was in the carry-on Tracy left with us, sitting innocuously in a closet. We'd discussed putting it in the hotel safe, but we didn't want to draw attention to ourselves.

As Tracy had said, the idea was to fly as far under the radar as we could.

I called a taxi service, and we waited outside the hotel for them to arrive. The driver was a disgruntled older man who had very little interest in customer service.

"Get in," he grunted, pushing the back door open by leaning over the front seat, rather than getting out to open it for us.

"Um, thank you," McKenzie said politely as we got in. She slid across the seat and grimaced.

I knew why when I got in after her. It was sticky!

"Where you going?" the driver asked impatiently before I could say anything about the seat.

"The nearest used car dealership," I replied.

He nodded and started into traffic even before we'd fastened our seat belts. The movement of the taxi made trash roll around the floor from the front seat. All in all, it was a disgusting ride.

We couldn't get to the dealership fast enough, in my opinion.

When we stopped, I all but leapt out of the car and pulled McKenzie out after me.

"Don't forget to pay me. I've got a baseball bat in here, you know," the driver growled.

"Oh! We weren't going to walk away. I just need to get some money out of my purse." She fished in the voluminous purse and pulled out a wallet that had about a hundred dollars in it. "How much?"

It was then I noticed he hadn't been running the meter. "Is the meter broken?" I asked, knowing full well he was about to try to take us for a ride.

"Yup." He smiled an oily smile. "Fifty bucks."

"That's too bad," I said, stopping her from pulling it out. "The way

I see it, you should be getting about twenty-five. And be very happy about it, because if that was a fifteen-dollar ride, I'd be very much surprised. Unless you want me to call the cab company."

The driver scowled at me. "Twenty-five, just because I like you."

"Uh-huh." I took my hand off her wrist so she could pay him.

"What about tip?" the driver asked.

"Don't push it," I replied flatly.

The driver spat on me, then sped away, flipping us off.

I made a face while McKenzie pulled tissues out of her purse and dabbed at the spit on my shirt. "Okay, that has to be the grossest experience I've ever had."

"Yeah," she agreed. "That was pretty gross."

"We're burning these clothes when we get back to the hotel, not washing them," I said.

"Probably a good idea." McKenzie turned to Earl's Emporium.

The lot was filled with all kinds of used vehicles, from motorcycles and trikes, to trucks and minivans. There was even a little blue Smart car. I wondered where to even begin.

I shouldn't have worried. A man in a suit spotted us like an eagle spotting prey and swooped over to us. "Hello. I'm Earl. Can I help you find something today?"

McKenzie smiled at him. "Hi. I'm Naomi, and this is my fiancé, Alex. We're looking for a used vehicle."

"One with four wheels that runs," I added, putting my arm around her.

Earl laughed. "If I had a nickel for every time I heard that! What's your budget?"

"About thirty-thousand," she said. It was the price we'd agreed upon at the hotel.

"Gotcha. Well, there are several vehic—wait, Naomi Johnson and Alex Clay?" he asked.

I tensed. "Yes."

"Oh! Your friend called and said she wanted to surprise you. Your RAV4 is almost ready. We're just finishing up detailing it for you," he said. "Lovely lady. I'm an honest man, so I'll tell you she paid a few thousand more than it was worth. I tried to tell her that, but she just said to have it detailed before you got here. I don't think either of us thought you'd show up so soon."

"Tracy Franz?" I assumed.

"That's her! Yeah, she said you keep your money. You guys need it. Whatever that means." He pulled out his phone. "Hey, Neil? Yeah, are you almost done with the RAV4? Okay, well, bring it around when you're finished. They're here already."

It was uncanny how Tracy knew we'd be going to this particular dealership. Then again, maybe she'd bought a car for us at every dealership from here to Duluth!

I shook myself. *No, her father would notice that much going out.*

Speaking of which….

"How did Tracy pay for the RAV4?" I asked cautiously. If she used a wire transfer, I hoped Morgan Franz was as dumb as she thought he was and wasn't paying attention to his daughter's strange purchases in Grand Marais.

"Cash. She and a nice girl named Gwendolyn stopped here in a convertible. Said they were on their way back to Mankato, but wanted to do something nice for some friends. I'll tell you something, if I had a friend like that, I'd thank my lucky stars," he said.

Relief washed over me. "I do thank my lucky stars for them both."

"It's beautiful!" McKenzie ducked out from under my arm to get a closer look at the charcoal gray RAV4 as it pulled up.

"Just like new. I know all salesmen say this, but it really was just driven by a lady with a hip problem to get groceries and back. Real low miles. Just two years old. Hybrid," Earl said proudly. "Now, if I could just see some ID?"

She and I both held out our brand new fake driver's licenses.

"Great," he said with a nod.

Neil—or at least I assumed it was Neil—walked past McKenzie to hand me the fob.

The look on her face was priceless and I had to bite my cheek not to laugh. "Thank you, both. We'll be on our way now."

"It's a pleasure doing business with you. Well, with Miss Franz, but you get what I mean," Earl chuckled.

Sulking, McKenzie got in the passenger side of the RAV4. "Misogyny is alive and well."

I did laugh then, tucking the fob into my pocket. "I might let you drive it to get groceries on Sundays," I teased.

She swatted me. "Just drive us back to the hotel."

"Yes, my love," I smiled.

WE KEPT OUR PHONES ON US AT ALL TIMES. TO SAVE MONEY, WE DIDN'T go out to eat, but made meals in our hotel room kitchen. The week was fast coming to a close, and we still hadn't heard anything from Tracy or Gwendolyn.

"Where do we go from here?" McKenzie asked me as we laid in bed, gazing out the window at Lake Superior.

"I don't know, honestly. Maybe Canada?" I said, stroking her hair.

"Maybe. We can't go too far, though. If an opportunity comes up, we want to be able to get back quickly," she pointed out.

"That's very true." It would have been such a nice moment, such a wonderful vacation—or even honeymoon—if we weren't in the trouble we were in. If family and friends weren't being held hostage, or God only knew what, by Ike.

She dropped her chin onto my chest. "Maybe Duluth?"

"Duluth would be a good option," I said. I rubbed her back, reveling in the feel of her naked skin against mine.

McKenzie frowned at me. "You're worried."

Damn. There was no point in lying to her. "I am. How can you tell?"

She poked me between the eyebrows. "You get a little line right here."

I laughed and captured her hand so I could nibble on her fingertips. "You're very observant."

"You're the love of my life. Of course I notice all the little things," she said.

My heart pounded, even while the rest of me completely melted. I touched her cheek tenderly. "You're the love of my life, too."

I needed to be with her. I needed to be *inside* her.

"You need it, too?" she whispered, pressing her lips to mine.

"Hell yes, honeybee," I responded.

I rolled her underneath me, kissing her and grazing my teeth over her neck. I began to reach down between us, but she captured my hand.

"I'm ready," she panted. "Please just be inside me."

I was glad it was just my brain that exploded because those were perhaps the seven sexiest words that had ever come out of her mouth. I was ready, too, so I joined our bodies with one powerful thrust.

McKenzie arched her back and let out a moan that traveled straight to my dick. Just like she said, she was ready—hot, wet, and still deliciously tight.

"I could die a very happy man right now, I swear," I groaned in her ear as I began pumping in and out of her.

"Don't do that! I haven't come yet!" she said breathlessly.

I chuckled and kissed her while our bodies found a rhythm we both liked. Soon, we were beyond words, just lost in the moment and in each other.

She took my hand and squeezed it, her breath coming in little gasps. She was close.

So was I.

"Honeybee, I love you," I managed, feeling her begin to clench around my cock.

"I-I love you, too!" she cried out, her teeth chattering from the force of her orgasm.

Her body milked mine for my cum, and my body was only too happy to oblige. I came hard, pushing as deep into her as I could go.

McKenzie wrapped her arms and legs around me as we came down. Her breasts rubbed against my chest.

As usual, my dick had not lost interest. I was still hard inside her. I wanted more. I needed more.

"You want to go again?" she asked, though it wasn't really a question.

"When have we ever just done it once?" I grinned.

She laughed. "It's because you're incorrigible."

I fondled her breast, thumbing her nipple. "You like that about me."

McKenzie gasped. "T-true."

I began thrusting again.

6

THE WAITING GAME

McKenzie

I wrapped myself around Will, biting his shoulder as he rode me hard. It still amazed me how much stamina he had. How much he wanted me. How much he *needed* me.

That was just fine, because I needed him, too.

I moved my hips with his, our sweaty bodies rubbing together deliciously.

He tugged my hair, and I backed off his shoulder only so that he could graze his teeth over my neck.

"Will," I moaned as he feasted on my skin, my hair still wound tightly around his fist.

"Tell me you love me," he growled in my ear.

My body was already heating up toward detonation, but his warm breath against my ear made me gasp and drove me even closer to the brink. "I love you," I said without hesitation.

"Tell me you're mine," he continued.

I panted. *What brought this on?* He usually wasn't so possessive.

But I did as he asked. "I'm yours."

He thumbed my clit and thrust powerfully one more time, tipping me right over the edge.

I clung to him, my body shuddering against his.

Will came hot inside me then. He groaned against my neck, his fist still firmly buried in my hair.

I sifted my fingers through his hair while he finished. "Will, what's wrong?" I asked.

"Does something need to be wrong?" he responded with a weak chuckle. He loosened his grip and began dropping little butterfly kisses wherever he could reach.

"Okay, then, what's right?" I countered, arching my back when he moved down my body to suck on my nipples.

"I want to get married," he said, catching me completely off guard.

I brought my head up and knocked my chin on the crown of his head. "What now?"

"Oof!" He stopped sucking my breasts and rubbed his head. "That was the plan, wasn't it?"

"It was Ike and your grandfather's plan. And don't get me wrong, I was a hundred percent on board with that part of the plan. I'd love to be your wife. But... you're like saying... right now?" I gaped.

"Yes. Right now. As in we throw some clothes on, go to the court-house, and get hitched," he said.

I blinked at him. "You know there are about a thousand things stopping that from happening, right?"

"I know. It's insane. But I want to. Desperately." He leaned up and kissed me. "I don't want to die without having married you."

"Die?! What are you talking about?!" I cried. "Do you have cancer or something?"

"No. But all these things that keep happening to us because of my grandfather's involvement in illegal businesses... I just want... I want to be your husband." He sighed. "It's a stupid idea."

I stroked his cheek. "I love you. I want to be your wife. But we don't have access to our real documents, and our fake identities don't have birth certificates. I don't think."

Will perked up suddenly. "We could contact that guy again. The one who made the fake IDs."

"You want a fake wedding certificate?" I asked, frowning.

"No. I want to see if he could do it for real." He sat up and patted around the bedside table for his burner phone.

"What are you doing?" I sat up as well.

"Texting Tracy. I want to know what her guy can do," he said.

I watched him start tapping a message out. "Okay… what do we do once we're married?"

"Celebrate," he replied without looking up.

"Celebrate? Celebrate how?"

He looked up then with a sexy grin on his face.

"We already do that! How is getting married right this second going to change anything? What's your hurry?" I demanded.

Will gave me a puppy-dog look. "Please just go along with it?"

My heart melted. *Damn him!* "Okay. I don't know what the rush is, but if you're sure this is what you want, and you need it now, then yes, I'm happy to be your wife."

"I really wanted to do some grand gesture on a beach at sunset with a ring," he sighed. "But… I just keep thinking we're running out of time."

"What's giving you that sense? I mean, Ike thinks we're dead. We're free-ish for a while. No one's crawling up our backs. This is the most peace we've had since I met you," I said.

He kissed me softly. "I think that's why. I don't know when this peace is going to end, and while we have it, I want to marry you."

"As long as we have a proper ceremony when we get my parents. And Shep and Dolly," I conceded.

"Of course. I wouldn't have it any other way." He kissed me again.

We laid back down, touching each other gently. We dozed off in each other's arms.

Then Will's phone rang. With a sleepy groan, he snatched it up.

We both looked at the screen, not recognizing the number.

"Hello?" Will said, cautiously answering. He put the phone on speaker. "Tracy?"

"You're a very hard man to find, as usual, Will," came Ike's unmistakable voice.

"Sonofabitch," Will hissed. He waved at me, pointing at our things.

"Unfortunately," Ike went on, "I don't know where you are right now. But I thought I might give you some extra incentive to come out of hiding."

There was a shriek in the background.

"Mom? Dolly?!" I gasped, frozen on the edge of the bed.

"Not so much. I mean, those would have been excellent choices, but I thought I'd punish one of the snoopy little bitches you sent my way," Ike said.

Will shook his head at me and pointed to our things again. He took the phone off speaker and put it to his ear so I couldn't hear Ike's side of the conversation. Or, and I was pretty sure this was his true motive, whatever they were doing to Gwendolyn or Tracy. "What do you want?" Will asked harshly.

I gestured to the phone, but Will shook his head again and pointed at our bags. With nothing else to do, I got out of bed, got dressed, and began packing our things.

Ike must have had a long list of wants, because I was almost finished packing and had laid one outfit out for Will by the time he responded. "You can't have that. Look, if this is a matter of signing over the company for you, then draw up the papers and I'll sign them. In a public place. But leave Gwendolyn alone."

Gwendolyn. I felt sick to my stomach. Tracy was the daughter of Morgan Franz, so she would have had some protection that way. But Gwendolyn?

They could do anything to Gwendolyn.

"What do you mean, 'that's not enough'? You don't even like me. Why would you want me running my grandfather's businesses? I'll sign whatever you want, just fuck off and leave our family and friends alone!" Will yelled.

I clutched the bag of money to my chest.

"Oh come on. You can't tell me you can't figure a way around some old madman's will," he scoffed at whatever Ike was saying.

There was a pause.

"That's not my fault. Do you think I wanted to go into the family business? No. So figure it out, Ike, and leave Gwendolyn alone!" he snapped.

Then there was a scream so loud I could hear it even though the phone wasn't on speaker.

I dropped the bag of money and scrambled across the bed, snatching the phone from Will. "Gwendolyn?!"

He tried to steal the phone back but I rolled out of his reach. "Ike, what did you do to Gwendolyn?"

"Bran thought it might be nice if they were a matching pair," Ike chuckled. "Nice to hear your voice, McKenzie. Maybe you can talk some sense into Will before we do worse things to people you love."

My hand shook. I could hear Gwendolyn choking in the background.

Choking?! "Ike, did any of it get down her throat?!" I asked.

Will plucked the phone from my shaking hand. Reluctantly, he put it back on speaker.

"You *fucking* idiot!" Ike shouted, sounding distant as though he'd taken the phone away from his mouth. "I said to *mar* her, not *kill* her!"

Bile rose in my throat. "Oh my God, Will. Oh my God."

He used his free arm to pull me against his chest, his grip almost crushing.

We heard a lot of scrambling, then what had to be Gwendolyn's last gurgle.

"Fuck." Ike let out a long sigh. "Well, at least Bran had the good sense God gave a goldfish to close his mouth."

Will's chest rose and fell with shallow breaths. Anger like I'd never sensed from him coated his next words. "Now, there will be no compromises."

"There were never going to be any compromises. Your grandfather's wishes were set down in iron. There's nothing I can do but bring you back in," Ike said testily.

"I'd suggest you save whatever money Grandfather was paying you and find a small tropical island somewhere. A place you can hide. Because I am going to kill you, Ike, if it's the last thing I do," Will seethed.

Ike snorted. "I'd love to see you pull that off."

"You will." He ended the call.

My whole body shook. I couldn't imagine the pain Gwendolyn had suffered up until the moment she died. "Oh my God."

"We've got to leave the phones, honeybee," he said gently. "And we've got to go. We'll go to Duluth, like you suggested. We'll get new phones, and we'll contact Tracy."

I couldn't breathe. I couldn't think. I couldn't move.

He gave me a little shake. "McKenzie, we have to go now."

"I... I...." I gripped his arm.

"*Now*, McKenzie," he said more firmly.

Tears rolling down my cheeks, I pulled away from him and went to grab the carry-on suitcase and my purse, both with cash in them.

Will got up and pulled on the outfit I'd set out for him.

We had one other carry-on with some clothes and essentials we'd purchased. He grabbed the handles of both carry-ons, leaving me holding my purse.

I felt completely numb, stumbling after him as though in a drunken haze.

He put the suitcases in the back of the RAV4 and helped me up into the passenger seat. Then, he started the SUV and pulled away from the hotel without bothering to check out.

"Naomi Johnson," I whispered, committing my new identity to memory. I wished I had her life. She sounded like she had such a nice, normal life.

We drove in silence for the whole two hours it took to get to Duluth. I couldn't stop shaking.

"I think this hotel will be good. I don't want us blowing all our money on luxury hotels," he finally said, pulling into a modest hotel from a well-known chain.

I didn't answer. I didn't know how.

"I'm going to go to the main office and see if we can get a room. You wait here. Oh, I'll need... let's just call it an even thousand dollars from your purse," he pressed.

When I didn't move, he tugged my purse off my shoulder and took the money out himself. With a heavy sigh, he kissed my forehead. "We'll talk about it when I get back. Well, when we get to the room. I'll order us a pizza, and we'll talk about it. Okay?"

Still trembling, I managed a nod.

Will stepped out of the RAV4 and locked me inside. I pointed a vent at me, hoping the air conditioning would make the cold sweats stop.

I didn't know how many minutes had passed, but he returned. He opened my door and I slid out, straight into his waiting arms.

"I'm sorry, honeybee," he said softly, brushing his lips over my hair. "I'm sorry. I'm sorry all these bad things keep happening. It's all my fault."

Still feeling stiff, I put my arms around his neck. "It's Ike's fault. And Masterson's fault. But it's not your fault. Don't say it is."

He tilted my chin up and kissed me. It was then I felt wetness against my cheeks. Except, I hadn't begun to cry yet.

Will was crying.

That made me burst into tears. "Will, when does this ever end?!"

He took a deep breath. "It ends when I end it. And it's going to end soon."

7

TRACY

WILL

"Just sleep for a while. I'm going to take care of some things. I'll be right back," I said, stroking McKenzie's hair as she laid in bed.

I expected her to argue, to insist she come with me. The fact that she didn't broke my heart. She was in a bad way.

"Oh, honeybee," I whispered, kissing her forehead and pulling the blanket up under her chin before heading out the door. I checked the handle three times to make sure no one could get in without a keycard. Then I headed down to the RAV4.

I got directions to the nearest place I could get pay-as-you-go phones. I bought two.

Next, I drove to a fast food restaurant and sat in the parking lot. Taking a leaf from McKenzie's book, I'd memorized Tracy's and Gwendolyn's phone numbers several days ago.

My jaw tightened as I realized I wouldn't need to remember Gwendolyn's anymore.

I took a deep breath and dialed Tracy, hoping against hope she wasn't also being subjected to torture.

"Hello?" Morgan Franz, her father, answered.

Not a good sign, but at least it wasn't Ike. "Is she all right?" I asked.

"Who is this?" Franz demanded.

"You know who this is." I waited for his answer.

"She's fine," Franz replied testily. "No thanks to you."

I ended the call. Before I could throw the phone out the window, however, he called back. I knew I should have ignored it, but Tracy had helped us and if there was anything I could do to reciprocate....

"Yes?" My voice was terse.

"You need to come in. You've ruined my daughter's life and almost ruined mine. And it's my money you're using to trot around doing God knows what," Franz told me. "Go make nice with Ike before he decides Tracy and I—especially Tracy—are not worth the trouble. I'm not like your grandfather. I'm nowhere near the top of the food chain. It will get to the point where I can't protect her anymore."

Anger bubbled up inside me. I knew it was anger I should have been directing at Ike, but right then, it came out sideways. "You decided to throw in your lot with a murdering, human trafficking, drug dealing, earth raping monster. You're the one who ruined your life *and* your daughter's. That your daughter decided to do the decent thing is the only redeeming feature your family has!"

Franz fell silent. "And what about you as his grandson benefitting all those years from his ill-gotten gains?"

"If I'd known, I'd have taken off years ago. Now, are we done talking?" I asked.

"You owe me," he hissed.

"I don't owe you shit," I snapped back.

"You owe me your life," he continued.

I snorted. "Right." *Why am I keeping this asshole on the phone? Wait, why is he keeping me on the phone?!*

"Motherfucker," I swore and ended the call. I turned off the phone and tossed it out the window.

Stupid. Stupid!

Quickly, I drove away to a different fast-food restaurant about a mile away. There, I picked up some food for McKenzie and me.

I drove back to the hotel and went to our room. I'd half expected the door to be ajar or to hear sounds of distress from inside. But everything was quiet.

Holding my breath, I tapped the keycard to the door and stepped inside. I set the food down on the desk and checked the bathroom, then behind the curtains, before engaging the safety latch on the door. Then, I sat down on the edge of the bed and checked on McKenzie.

She was sleeping, though the expression on her face indicated she wasn't having good dreams.

That being the case, I didn't see a problem with waking her up to eat. "Honeybee…." I stroked her cheek. "Let's eat, my love."

McKenzie jerked, her eyes flying wide open. She looked at me without recognizing me for a moment, then relaxed and wrapped her arms around my waist, snuggling her head into my lap. "Will."

"Yes, honeybee. It's Will." I combed my fingers through her hair. "I brought something to eat. I thought we should eat it while it's hot. Fast food isn't that good after being microwaved."

"Is Tracy okay?" she asked, not moving from my lap.

Perceptive as always. "Tracy is fine. Her father's a bit pissed off at me, but he said he's managed to protect her."

"He had her phone," she inferred.

"Yes."

"How are we going to help her?" She looked up at me, her eyes red-rimmed but determined.

I sighed. "I don't know yet. Morgan Franz wants me to come in and do what Ike wants. But that's not exactly an option."

"No, it's not," she agreed.

"So," I said, "for now—food."

"Okay. I'm not hungry, but… I know it won't help anything if I starve myself." She slowly let go of me and sat up.

I went and brought the food over to the bed, perching on the edge once more as we ate burgers and fries that neither of us really tasted.

"I think hearing Gwendolyn die is the most horrible thing that's happened so far. And a lot of horrible things have happened," she said quietly.

I gathered up the trash from our little picnic and threw it away.

When I returned, I kicked off my shoes and got into bed with her, wrapping her in my arms. "A lot of horrible things *have* happened."

"She must have been in so much pain," she whispered.

"I know. I won't try to tell you she wasn't." I rubbed her back. "I wish I could make it so you didn't hear that. I was… I was trying… by taking the phone off speaker, but that wasn't the right thing to do, either."

"No. It wasn't." She buried her face in my neck and I felt my brave little soldier's tears on my skin.

In that moment, I was happy my grandfather was dead and only regretted that Ike wasn't. It was a situation I had every intention of fixing as soon as possible.

"I'm going to make it okay," I promised her again.

"How?" she sniffled. "How can you possibly do that?"

I was quiet for a moment. "Give me the weekend to think about it. If all else fails, I'll go back to the business and play nice until I find a window of opportunity. But I'd like to avoid that, if possible."

"We can't go back," she argued. "We'll never get out! Not any of us."

I kissed her hair. "*You* won't ever be going back."

Her head came up. "What's that supposed to mean?"

"Honeybee." I thumbed the tears off her cheeks. "I couldn't possibly take you with me. Not into that kind of danger."

McKenzie's eyes widened.

Then she slapped me.

I winced, though I'd kind of been expecting it. "Ow."

"William Masterson the Third! Don't you *dare* go wandering back into that situation without me!" she shouted.

"Shh. We might have neighbors," I murmured, working my jaw. She did pack a strong punch.

She scowled at me, but lowered her voice. "Never, ever, *ever* try to tell me you're leaving me behind in any of this. I swear I will stick to you like moss. You're never getting rid of me!"

"I don't want to get rid of you. I want to protect you," I sighed. "And I'm going to."

"What, is this you putting your foot down?" she asked.

"Yes." I didn't know then that this one word was the worst answer given in the history of mankind.

McKenzie slapped me again.

"I'm starting to lose my sense of humor about getting hit in the face," I grumbled, rubbing my cheek.

"Tough. I don't know if you know this, William Masterson the Third, but you've really put your foot in it this time. And I'm this close to ramming mine right up your ass!" She scrambled up and folded her arms, looking down at me. "You don't get to go full on hero mode on me, treating me like I'm some damsel in distress. I don't know how many times I have to say this, but we're a team! You don't leave your teammate behind."

I sat up as well. "McKenzie, listen to me...."

"No, *you* listen to *me*. We're going to figure this out together. So, this weekend, while your big brain is thinking about what we can do, you're going to include me," she insisted. Then, she leaned in and said menacingly. "And if Big Willy ever wants to get lucky again, you're going to apologize for being a dickhead."

I knew she was serious, but her last sentence had me choking back a laugh. "'Big Willy'?"

"Shut up. You know that wasn't my point." She blushed.

"Well, Big Willy might be a bit disappointed, but I love you more than sex," I said. "I'm not sorry for wanting to protect you from *my* mess."

"It's *our* mess," she replied. "Don't get it twisted."

"But I dragged you into it to begin with," I tried to explain.

"Yeah, because Masterson totally wasn't watching my family like goldfish the whole time we were living on the farm," she scoffed. "I mean, he was absolutely going to leave us alone to live long, happy lives."

She had a point, but I wasn't ready to let it go yet. "Yes, but he was *my* grandfather."

"Please. That ship sailed the second he made my mother carry you.

Argue all you want, butthead, but I'm going to be able to counter every one of your points," she said.

"Butthead?" I snorted.

"That's right. You're being a butthead." She scowled at me.

"And a dickhead," I reminded her.

"That, too." She raised her chin. "And if you want to get any kind of head in the future, you're going to stop being both."

I sighed. "McKenzie. I won't be able to concentrate on what I have to do if I'm worried about you being in danger all the time. Besides, this is all hypothetical, at this point."

"Then hypothetically remove your head from your ass because there's no way I'm letting you do any of this without me. It's *my* parents' and *our* friends' lives at stake. I'm not going to sit in a hotel for weeks or months or, God forbid, *years* twirling my hair and hoping everything turns out all right. No. No way," she said.

I considered sneaking off into the night once she'd gone to sleep, if I had to return to Ike. But I knew she'd lose her shit and do something crazy like call Ike herself. "You can be a real pain in the ass, I just need you to know that," I muttered.

"You love my ass." She smiled triumphantly.

"That I do. But I love you more." I was still frustrated, but I had to kiss her. Her smile was just too tempting.

McKenzie wrapped her arms around me and deepened the kiss. I groaned and slid my hands up under her shirt.

"Say it," she murmured against my lips.

"Say… what?" I asked hazily.

"Say you're sorry for being a dickhead," she said.

I wanted to lie to her. I wanted to lie to her so badly. Big Willy was about to be *very* disappointed. "I'm not sorry for wanting to protect you."

She pouted. "Well, that sucks." Then, she detangled herself from me and laid down on the bed with her back to me.

Yes, Big Willy was very disappointed. It took herculean effort, but I managed to ask, "Do you want me to sleep in the bathtub?"

"No," she replied angrily. "We're just not going to have sex."

"Okay." I laid down beside her and folded my hands behind my head. I stared at the ceiling.

McKenzie made a frustrated sound and tugged on my wrist until I was spooning her with an arm around her.

"So, not having sex, but still going to cuddle?" I asked.

"I never said anything about cuddling," she replied mutinously.

8

NOT SO SNUGGLY

McKenzie

I'd never been so sexually frustrated in my life. Not even when my first boyfriend only went as far as touching my knee when we made out in high school.

I really, really wanted Will to pound me until I couldn't remember my own name. But I also wanted him to realize the error of his ways and to stop trying to take everything on himself.

So, frustration it was.

I wasn't coming, so sleep wasn't, either. I thought about sending him to the bathtub or at least wriggling out of his arms. But both possibilities would have just made the whole situation worse.

"Are you ready to admit defeat?" Will asked, his breath warm against my shoulder.

Oh hell *no!* "I will die on this hill," I said stubbornly.

"That'd be a shame," he replied.

I turned in his arms, glowering at him. Unfortunately, it was so dark from the blackout curtains he couldn't see me glower, but I was definitely glowering. "You need to get over yourself."

He laughed! "I don't think I'm going to agree with you anytime soon. We can't just agree to disagree?"

"No!" I poked him in the chest. "You're taking it all on yourself again, and that's not okay. We're a *team*."

"So… we're just going to keep circling back to the same argument, I guess," he sighed.

"I guess so." I pouted because I knew he couldn't see it. My eyes might have gotten a little dust in them as well.

"I can feel you pouting," he said.

I frowned. "I'm not pouting."

"You are."

"Fine. I might be. So what? I'm very angry with you right now," I mumbled.

"Honeybee…" he began.

I rolled back to my other side. "Nope. Don't want to hear it. Unless it's an apology."

Will sighed. "All right. Sleep well."

"You, too," I grunted back.

Silence fell. Minutes ticked by. Then, an hour at least.

"You're not asleep, are you?" I said into the darkness.

"No," he replied.

"Great." Sarcasm dripped from my tone.

He chuckled. "I guess neither of us are getting much sleep tonight. Want to watch some TV instead?"

"Might as well," I agreed. We sat up, and he turned on a lamp while I grabbed the remote. "What's on at this time of night, anyway?"

"Horror flicks and news," he said.

We looked at each other. "News," we decided in unison.

I turned on a news channel so we could watch fifth-string reporters recap what had happened the day before. As usual, it was depressing, but at least nothing with a knife was popping out from behind closed doors. That was a little too close to home for me.

I yawned.

Will grabbed my shoulder. "Shit."

"What?" I asked, looking around, my adrenaline pumping.

He gestured to the TV. "Watch the bottom of the screen."

I did. And my stomach dropped in horror.

BILLIONAIRE BRAN LOCKWOOD ENGAGED TO HEIRESS TRACY FRANZ.

It scrolled two or three times before my brain could fully process it. I felt like slime had been dumped over me. I couldn't imagine how Tracy felt.

"We have to do something!" I said, digging my nails into Will's thigh.

"I agree," he responded. "We should pack up and head back to Minnetonka right now. If we start now, we should be there by sunup"

I looked up at him. "No arguing that I should stay here and wait?"

"Would you stay here and wait?" He raised an eyebrow.

"No."

"Then there's really no point in arguing, is there?" he snorted.

"I'm glad you're finally seeing things my way." I got out of bed and started packing.

Will helped, getting our toiletries from the bathroom and making sure we had the bag of Tracy's money and my purse. "All set?" he asked.

I ran my hands over my rumpled clothes and nodded. "All set."

We got in the RAV4 and began driving south.

"What are we going to do when we get there?" I asked.

He rubbed the back of his neck. "I don't know yet."

"Maybe we should stake out her house. Or Bran's. Or both?" I suggested.

"I think it might be safer to stake out Tracy's house. But I have a bad feeling that Ike is hoping we'll do just that." He shook his head. "I don't know what we're going to do, honestly. I just can't in good conscience leave her there alone without anyone to turn to."

"I feel the same way." I wracked my brain for ideas. Then, I remembered. "Tracy shops regularly at Princess House of Fashion."

Will paused, then nodded. "We'll stake that out, then."

"I'll stake it out. You'll wait with the getaway vehicle," I said. "I think you'll be recognized."

"We've both been in some very large engagement announcements," he reminded me.

I bit my lip. "True."

"But I suppose you're right. I've been on the circuit my whole life. You've been in just a few pictures, comparatively." He let out a long, frustrated breath. "I don't think we have a choice if we want to save her."

"We definitely have to save her," I said. "She risked so much for us! And, you know, *Bran*...." I shuddered.

"Yes, let us not forget that asshole," he replied darkly.

"Should we maybe just kill him and let Tracy's father continue to protect her? It's not like we have a really sophisticated operation here," I mumbled.

"Don't think it hasn't crossed my mind. But no, Ike will just find some other way to use her. And honestly, I think if we killed Bran, we'd be doing my grandfather's buddies a favor. They don't think much of his intelligence," he said. "I hate the guy, but if him still being around is a hindrance to their operation, well, I guess I can wait."

I nodded slowly. "Good point."

"So, we're risking the boutique." He sounded miserable.

"I won't get hurt," I promised. "I'll be really careful."

"The second part, I believe. We don't have a whole lot of control over the first," he sighed.

I put my hand on his thigh. "I know that makes you crazy."

"You have no idea," he replied.

"We have to do this," I reiterated.

"We do," he agreed. He put his hand over mine.

I took a deep breath. "If I get caught, you have to let me go."

Will's head snapped around. "Pardon?!"

"Driving. *Driving!*" I reminded him, pointing to the road.

He turned his attention back to the road. Luckily, we'd only swerved a little. "What nonsense are you talking about now?"

"I'm saying that if I get caught in the boutique, you need to *not* get caught and you *can't* turn yourself in to Ike because you need to figure out a way to get us out. And licking Ike's boots until the day he dies is not the way that's going to get done," I said.

Will scowled at the road. "You'd better not get caught because my very next stop will be the Masterson building."

I swatted his shoulder. "It most certainly will not!"

"Watch me."

"I'm telling you, going back under Ike's thumb is not the answer!" I cried.

He glanced at me. "If I'd gone down to Minnetonka without you, snuck out in the middle of the night, you would have stood in the middle of the road waving your arms and demanded to be brought to Ike."

I pursed my lips. "That's not the point."

"It is the point." He sighed. "Let's face it. We're both willing to do really crazy, stupid things to protect each other. So, the only solution here is: you can't get caught."

"Okay. Then I won't," I said.

"Okay."

We fell into another silence.

"But if I do get caught…" I finally blurted.

Will groaned and tightened his grip on the steering wheel. "Then we're getting married in a big ceremony full of stuff we don't like and people we don't know. Well, people I only consider acquaintances and you don't know at all. Bran will probably be my best man."

I made a strangled sound in my throat. "The hell he will!"

"So, don't get caught," he said firmly.

"But…."

"Don't. Get. Caught," he repeated.

There was no other choice, it seemed. Not if I didn't want Bran in my wedding party. "Okay. I'll do my best."

He gave my temple a quick kiss. "I know you will."

We drove until dawn. The sun came up, bright and beautiful. Hopeful, even.

As we pulled into the parking lot of yet another modest hotel, I hoped the sun wasn't lying.

"I'll check us in," Will said. "Lock the doors. We don't need anything else to happen."

"Yeah, a carjacking is just what we need right now," I groaned.

His lips brushed over mine, then he grabbed some money from my purse and headed in to the front desk.

I leaned my head back against the headrest. I must have dozed off, because the next thing I knew, Will was knocking on the window.

"Sorry," I said, quickly unlocking the SUV. "I think I fell asleep."

He smiled at me. "I'm glad. I think we've got some time to catch a few winks. Boutiques like that only open at eleven."

"Oh thank God," I replied. "I'm so tired, and you were driving so you must be exhausted."

"Eh, more sexually frustrated than anything," he said.

"Well, you're not alone there, either," I grumbled.

Will held out his hand and when I took it, he pulled me out of the RAV4 and into his arms. "Why don't we forget our differences for a little while. You can die on your hill later. Or hopefully not at all."

I hesitated. "But I'm mad at you."

"Make-up sex?" he suggested, waggling his eyebrows.

I rolled my eyes. "I feel like I'm giving a kid a toy after he threw a tantrum. Not a good precedent to set."

"I'll remember that when we have our own kids." He reluctantly let me go and grabbed our two suitcases.

Our own kids?! My cheeks heated up. I hadn't given it much consideration, since we were always in dire situations. And I needed to think about college. But now that I thought about it….

"Do you like that idea?" he asked softly.

"Kids?" I gulped.

He nodded. "Yes."

I licked my lips, which had suddenly gone dry. "Yes. I do."

"Good. I'm glad." He smiled softly at me.

I shouldered my purse, trying to remember I was mad at him. "I mean it, though. I don't like that you were going to try to make decisions without me and go off on your own."

"I mean it, too, when I say I want to protect you. And I'm not sorry for wanting to try. But I feel as though I'm cutting off my nose to spite my face here. If I apologize, I won't mean it, and that's not fair to you. On the other hand, if I never get to touch you again, I'm going to die," he said.

Will was right. We were never going to get anywhere in this argument. We'd each drawn our line in the sand, and neither of us was budging.

"Make-up sex, huh?" I sighed.

"I think so, yes," he responded.

"I guess… that would be okay," I said grudgingly.

He grinned. "Don't sound so excited about it."

"Maybe I should just say I won't give you any more blowjobs," I mused, trying to think of a proper punishment that didn't involve endless sex deprivation on my part.

Will chuckled. "If you say so." He began rolling the suitcases into the hotel.

"Hey, I can stop anytime I want!" I insisted as I followed him.

"You make it sound as though you're a drug addict," he laughed. "Though I'm one to talk. I'm definitely addicted to you."

"As well you should be!" We crowded into a small elevator and went up to the second floor.

He leaned over and kissed my neck, sending a zing of desire all the way down to my toes. "I'll bet I can get you to blow me."

I shivered. "Fat chance, buddy."

"In fact, I know I can. Shall we test that theory?" he whispered in my ear.

"You can try all you want. It's not gonna happen," I said, folding my arms over my chest.

"Uh-huh." The elevator stopped, and we went to our room.

Where I did, indeed, end up blowing him.

9

STAKE-OUT

I didn't like it. I didn't like it one bit.

We'd traded the RAV4 for a nondescript, white Silverado. Just in case Tracy had been forced to disclose which vehicle we were driving.

It was the best we could do, given the circumstances. The circumstances being parked about a block from her house, just within view of the gate, trying to track the comings and goings of those within.

"We should stake out the boutique instead," I said for the thousandth time.

"We tried that," McKenzie reminded me. Again. "We were outside that place for two weeks. Maybe they're just not letting her out?"

"I don't know that we're going to find an opportunity to go in," I murmured, my eyes on the gate as it opened.

"Would that even be safe?" she asked.

"No." A sleek, silver Aston Martin slipped out through the wrought iron gap.

We both sat up, then ducked back down as the car turned our way.

I kept an eye trained on the Aston Martin and as it passed, I swore. "It's just Morgan Franz."

"Her father?" She popped her head up as the Aston Martin drove away.

"Just him, his chauffeur, and a bodyguard." I smacked my hand on the steering wheel in frustration. "Hell."

McKenzie rubbed the back of her neck. "I suppose there's too many other people on the property to just go in and get her." She glanced at the glove compartment.

'Alex Clay' and 'Naomi Johnson' had also gotten themselves two handguns.

"At this point, Franz will have trained bodyguards keeping Tracy under lock and key. We're not exactly a match for them," I said, frustrated.

"Damn." Her face scrunched up and I knew she was thinking hard. I hoped that big brain of hers would come up with something actionable.

There was a knock on the truck window.

I jumped.

McKenzie opened the glove compartment and reached for a gun.

"Now, McKenzie, I'd suggest you not do that," a big, beefy man with a gun of his own said, staring us both down the barrel of it.

Where did he come from?!

"Will, I'm going to need you to roll down the window and hand those guns out to me. Slowly," the man continued, his gaze, and his gun, unwavering.

Fuck. Fuck. Fuck. *Fuck. Fuck!* I glanced at her.

Her hand was trembling over a gun.

I wondered if it was best to go down in a blaze of glory.

"Will?" Tracy's head came into view around the man's shoulder. She had a gun to her head.

"Roll down the window, Will," the burly guy repeated with infinite patience.

I looked at McKenzie again, who nodded, looking defeated. I rolled down the window.

"Guns. One at a time. Two fingers on the butt. Slowly," he instructed.

I took them out one at a time and handed them out to him. He passed them to a man standing nearby. I could see four of them, black-clad and beefy, in total.

"How did I not see you?" I asked angrily.

"Because you've been focused on that house for two weeks." He didn't laugh about it or call me an idiot. It was just a matter-of-fact statement.

McKenzie sought my hand, gripping it hard. "We won't go back to Ike Freeborn. You're gonna have to shoot us."

"Freeborn? Why would we take you to Freeborn? He doesn't pay his debts," he said.

I frowned. "What do you mean? Will you please stop threatening to shoot Tracy. Just let her go. I know we're the real targets."

"I'm not leaving!" Tracy insisted, even though there was a gun to her head.

"What do you mean, 'he doesn't pay his debts'?" McKenzie asked. "He's got more money than God. There's no reason for him *not* to pay you."

"Wrong." The bulky man gestured. "Let's go somewhere more private and discuss this further."

"We don't have to go to the second location," I whispered, knowing it was something drilled into female victims all the time. *Never go to the second location.*

McKenzie was thinking again. "I think we should hear them out. We aren't going to be any less dead here or there."

"I like her," he smiled.

I scowled at him. "We'll go with you, but you really need to let Tracy go."

"No can do. Her dad owes us, too. According to Freeborn," he said. He stepped back a few feet. "Lean out the window and open your door from the outside with your right hand.

I did as I was told. The door swung open.

He pointed to a black Escalade two cars back from us. "We're heading that way."

I stepped out of the Silverado and held my arms out to McKenzie.

She jumped down, and I put an arm around her as we walked to the Escalade.

The man shut the Silverado's door. Then all seven of us piled into the Escalade.

Tracy, McKenzie, and I crowded into the middle seat, while two men in black suits sat behind us and the other two got in the front. The man who held a gun on McKenzie and me took the passenger seat, while the one who'd been holding Tracy hostage drove.

"Is this a private enough place to talk?" I asked.

"Certainly," the man said. "We can start talking here."

"Great. What do you want?" I demanded.

He turned his head to look at us. "Like I said, we want to get paid. Ike Freeborn enlisted our services to get you from that cabin, and we got three people, but when it came time to pony up, he didn't have the funds."

"You know I don't have jack diddly, either, right?" I sighed. "You'd have been better off getting Tracy to crack her dad's safe."

"She did. There wasn't a penny in it." He shook his head. "Seems your grandfather's operation has taken quite a hit. But we finally figured it out."

"Figured what out?" I asked.

He grinned at me. "It all comes down to you, Will."

The women looked at me in confusion. I felt exactly the same way. "I don't understand."

"I'm sure you don't. I'll bet it's the last thing Freeborn wanted you to know," he chuckled.

"Still don't know what you're talking about," I said. McKenzie cuddled closer into me, and I tightened my arm around her.

Tracy just looked bewildered. "Are these people sane?" she mouthed to me.

All I could do was shrug.

"We're perfectly sane." He sobered. "Since your grandfather died, Freeborn has lost access to your grandfather's funds. He'd already been using his own to chase you down for months, since your grandfather decided he was going to be responsible for getting you back, or he was going to lose his job. So, he's tapped out. Maybe he has something tied up in the Cayman Islands, I don't know. What I do know is he doesn't have anything liquid to pay us with right now."

"Um… I'm not sure what Ike may have told you… under duress." I knew Ike must have been tortured. These were serious people, after all. The plan now was to make sure we weren't subjected to the same. "But… I don't exactly have access to my grandfather's money, either."

"That's what he wants you to think." He sounded smug.

I blinked. "I… can… access Grandfather's money?"

"You could throw it in your estate's pool and swim in it, if you wanted to," he said. "After you pay us, of course."

"Will?" McKenzie whispered.

"Will, keep them on retainer. We need guys on our side," Tracy spoke in a rush.

"How… exactly… am I supposed to access Grandfather's funds?" I asked. "Did Ike say?"

"I like that retainer idea. Basically, you just walk into your grandfather's lawyer's office and fill out the official paperwork. He's dead. You're the heir. Congratulations," he said.

I stiffened. "This sounds like a trap."

"Trap. Definitely," Tracy agreed. "Forget what I said about a retainer."

"Ike probably lied to you," McKenzie sighed. "I'm so sorry. This whole time, he's been pushing to get Will back into the office. There's probably some kind of clause that's going to say he has to sacrifice a baby under an oil spill or something horrible like that."

"Oh, Ike wasn't lying. I don't know what other stipulations or expectations there are, but Will can just walk in and take what's his." He frowned. "And that's exactly what he's gonna do."

Tracy threw her light blonde, beach waves hair over her shoulder and stabbed an expensively-manicured finger in his direction. "Listen here. I will find a way to get you your money, but none of us are going to get involved in human trafficking and arms dealing. Not for anybody."

I'd never quite seen her before these last few weeks. She'd just been another trophy-wife-to-be in a gaggle of trophy-wives-to-be. But there was a lot more to Tracy than met the eye. It kind of made me sad we were going to die before McKenzie and I could properly get to know our new friend. "I can't do what my grandfather did. If that's one of the stipulations, then I'm walking out of that lawyer's office without any money. I'm sorry."

"You're walking out of that lawyer's office with at least two-point-five million dollars," he said sternly. "It's non-negotiable. I'm sorry your grandfather was an asshole, but that's not our problem. Besides, don't you at least want to check and be sure what the paperwork actually says before we blow your brains out?"

McKenzie made an angry sound.

"Don't think I've forgotten about you, little missy. We're keeping you right here in the car while your boyfriend gets his inheritance squared away. If he fails, you die first," he growled.

"I said I'll get you your money!" Tracy yelled.

He turned to her. "And how do you expect to do that?"

"John Anders. I know he squirrels away a lot of money. He's always boasting about how when we're all down on our luck, he's going to be fine because he has gold. There's a safe in his office—" Tracy began.

"Were you a cat burglar in another life?" I asked, staring at her.

"Please. You should always be cautious of people who *say* they have money. I saw *Game of Thrones*," Tracy sniffed.

"Right... okay, so we're going to be able to break into Anders' house and grab his gold?" I said dubiously.

Tracy gestured to the men in the car. "We have friends."

"If we have to pull off a heist, it's gonna cost you," he grunted. But he did look intrigued.

Thank God. "You can have everything that's in the damn house, if you want. We just want to be left alone," I stated.

"Not everything. We want a million each to make a fresh start. So that's three million for us and everything else is for you," Tracy said logically.

"What if we decide what he's got isn't enough?" he asked.

"Well then, I guess we're all screwed," Tracy replied.

"Fair enough." He turned to the driver. "Let's go stake out the Anders Estate."

The driver grinned. "Sounds like a lot more fun than sitting outside some stuffy lawyer's office." He turned the Escalade around with a loud squeal of tires at the next intersection.

I looked at Tracy. "You are seriously diabolical. You are *wasted* as a debutante."

"Tell my father that, will you?" She responded with a touch of bitterness.

McKenzie reached across me to squeeze her hand. "Thank you, Tracy. For everything."

"Well, don't thank me yet," she mumbled.

"Why not?" McKenzie asked.

"Because, I wasn't expecting my dad's safe to be empty, either," Tracy said.

10

SAFECRACKER

McKenzie

Two other black SUVs met us at the Anders Estate. I wondered if my parents had ever had my same thought—why were they always *black*?!

The men in black suits got out of the SUVs in one choreographed movement. Seriously, it could have been a ballet.

I could see a guard in the guard station reaching under the desk. "Pretty sure the cops are coming," I warned.

"Pretty sure they're not." The man who'd been speaking to us gestured to someone outside the Escalade.

A few paces down there was a kind of electrical box. There was a man holding a chainsaw next to it. He nodded in our direction and completely decapitated the thing.

The guards then started going for their cell phones.

Another man in black pressed what I had to assume was some kind of sticky explosive to the glass and the guards froze.

The man simply stared them down.

They tumbled out of the guard booth with their hands raised.

The gate opened and those who were not occupied with the

guards drove inside. We stopped as a convoy right outside John Anders's front door.

"You can get out of the car now," our main contact said.

"So, just in case we get into trouble in there, is there something we can call you other than 'guy in the black suit'? Because there seems to be a lot of you all of a sudden," Will asked.

He chuckled. "Gray. Just Gray."

"Gray." Will climbed over me so he could help both Tracy and me out of the Escalade.

"Let's go say 'hello,'" Gray said, motioning for us to precede him.

I figured that meant they wanted *us* to do the honors of knocking on Anders's door.

I was right. "Go on," Gray prodded.

Will took a deep breath, then rang the security bell.

"No way we get out of here without the police showing up," I muttered.

"Ye of little faith." Gray winked.

The door didn't open right away. But then, a shaking maid appeared. "Please leave Diego alone," she begged.

"Is he one of the guards?" I asked, my stomach sinking.

She nodded. "My husband."

"Of course he is," Gray simpered. "All you have to do is be a good girl and let us in. Oh, and has anyone called the police yet?" His tone turned dark. "Don't lie to me."

She hung her head. "Yes."

"How many?" Gray pressed.

"At least three," she said.

Gray nodded. "Then I think you'd best bring me to Mr. Anders."

She winced. "He's in his panic room, sir."

"Well, that's inconvenient." Gray tapped his chin. "I suppose we'll have to find a way to get him out." His gaze fell on Will, Tracy, and me.

"We're not even his family! Why would he come out?!" Tracy protested as the maid began leading us to Anders's panic room.

"Because I know something you don't know," Gray grinned.

"What's that?" Will asked.

Gray just laughed. "I don't want to ruin the surprise."

The maid dropped us off in front of a wall in Anders's large suite. "He's in there," she said.

"Great." Gray put a hand on Will's shoulder…

… Then shoved him to his knees and put a gun to his head.

I couldn't stop a scream and made a grab for Will, but Tracy held me back.

"No! He might shoot him by accident!" she exclaimed.

I glared accusingly at Gray. "You sonofabitch."

Gray ignored me. "Come on out, John," he said sweetly. "You wouldn't want me to kill the golden goose, now would you?"

There was no response.

Gray audibly cocked his gun.

"No, please!" I begged, struggling against Tracy. She proved to be stronger than I expected.

"It's okay, McKenzie. Don't do anything," Will said. He was holding very, very still.

Don't do anything?! I was going to clock Tracy and jump on Gray in five seconds if—

The wall slid open. John Anders reluctantly stepped out. "I told the police we've had a security system malfunction and that it startled the staff."

"Excellent." Gray grabbed Will's arm and drew him back to his feet. He kept the gun on his temple, however.

"What's going on?!" I shouted, my heart squeezing even as Will stood calmly with the gun to his head.

"Do you want to tell her, or should I?" Gray asked Anders.

Anders sighed. "The accounts where we funnel the money from… Masterson's businesses… have all been locked. This was set to happen upon his death. None of us are getting paid anymore." He glared at Gray. "I would like that to change."

"What does that have to do with Will?! Please, just leave him alone!" I begged.

"Leave *us* alone," Tracy added. "We don't want any part in any of this. We're just here for the gold and then we're getting out of here!"

"Now you want my gold?" Anders snorted. "Fat chance. You'll have to shoot me first."

Gray turned the gun on Anders. "That won't be a problem."

Anders paled. He held up his hands. "Listen. Listen to me! You don't want to have to haul around a bunch of gold coins, trying to figure out how to get it all melted down and sold. No, you want to get paid. I know Ike couldn't pay you. I'm sorry about that. But, I mean, you're holding an infinite ATM right there."

"He's less than willing to step up," Gray said. "You're the alternative. Now hurry up and get us that gold. I'm fed up with all the 'you're gonna have to kill me's' I've heard today."

"Who even... Tracy." Anders scowled at her. "You really are a huge pain in the ass. I don't know why your father didn't just let Ike have you."

"Guess he loves me, in his own way," Tracy replied sweetly. "So... yeah. We were getting a couple big bags full of gold?"

"We were," Gray agreed. He gestured with his gun. "Let's go, Mr. Anders."

Anders grumbled under his breath and led us downstairs to a study that smelled slightly of cigars. Will looked immediately uncomfortable in his surroundings.

I wondered if this was where they'd forced him to help with the operation.

Anders went to one wall of bookshelves and pressed. The shelves swung out and revealed a large safe.

"Nice," Gray complimented him. "I'm going to get one just like this in my home."

"It's not cheap," Anders said, pressing his thumb to the biometric lock.

"I don't think money is going to be a problem," Gray chuckled.

The door clicked, and Anders paused with his hand on the handle. "Will, I think you should sit down before you faint."

Gray snorted, but Will sank into a chair regardless. I ran to his side, and so did Tracy, all of us huddled around that one leather chair.

Anders reached into the safe. "Just have to deactivate something so we all don't get blown to hell."

"Be my guest," Gray said, taking a step forward.

It was the last step he ever took. Anders swung the door wide open and pulled out a huge gun.

Gray's lips formed a startled O just before his head was completely blown away.

"Get upstairs!" Anders barked, waving us out the door. "Quickly!"

Not knowing what else to do, we listened to the man with the big gun and ran up the stairs.

Having heard the shots, some of the men in black suits came out of other areas and pulled their guns.

I wasn't sure what Anders had been in another life, but three of them were dead before we made it to the upstairs landing.

"The panic room!" Anders ordered. "Now, now, now!"

Will put an arm around me and grabbed Tracy by the wrist, hurrying us along. We tumbled into the panic room just before Anders. He closed the door just as gunshots rang out.

They peppered the outside wall, but it was nothing more dangerous than rain on a tin roof for those of us within.

Anders panted, then set the gun within easy reach and picked up his phone. "Yes. This is John Anders again. I'm afraid we really are under threat here. They seem to be professionals. If you could send a S.W.A.T. team, that would probably be best."

Will pulled us to the other side of the room from him and put himself between Tracy and me, and Anders. "I'm not—"

"Let me explain something to you, Will," Anders said, sitting down, gun still close by. "You're going to have all of us on your tail until the end of time unless you go in and take your inheritance. Do you really want that?"

"I don't like what comes with that inheritance," Will replied angrily. "I'm not going to rape the world just so you guys can keep making money off of sin."

"You don't even know what the terms are yet. None of us do. For all you know, all you have to do is go in, sign some paperwork, release the accounts to us, and go on your merry way," Anders pointed out.

"Right. Because Grandfather would have set it up that way," Will scoffed.

Anders shrugged. "You don't know until you find out for yourself."

"Even if I did get control of those accounts—which I doubt—I would never give that money to you willingly," Will said.

Anders laughed. "At least you're honest."

"Could we be less honest and more get-out-of-here motivated?" Tracy grumbled.

"It's not as though it was a revelation. John knew I wasn't going to just roll over. Didn't you, John?" Will replied.

"Of course I knew. But we're all in a pickle until you start signing paperwork... and it just so happens I have two very good reasons right here for you to do so," Anders said.

Will looked back at Tracy and me. "I guess you have me by the balls, don't you?"

"Pretty sure I do. But you've been in this position before, and miraculously managed to escape. I like my head right where it is, thank you very much." Anders glanced at the security feed on the wall. "Looks like the police are here."

"We can just leave with them," I said. "You can't keep us here. What are you going to do? Hold us at gunpoint in front of the police?"

"Tempting, but no. As far as they know, I'm the only person in here," Anders smirked.

"They're going to want you to come out." Will arched an eyebrow at him. "What will you do then?"

Anders shrugged. "I guess we all take our chances."

We watched the screens and waited for the police to clear the house. Once the coast was clear, Anders opened the panic room door.

"Help!" I yelled, running up behind him. "Help! He has a gun!"

"Is there somebody in there with you, John?" a plainclothes officer asked. I assumed he was a detective or a higher-up of some kind.

"Just some troublesome kids," Anders responded. "Honestly, they can be such a headache."

"We've been kidnapped!" I insisted.

The plainclothes officer turned to the three other officers behind him. "Forget you heard that. Go see about cleaning up downstairs."

"Yes, sir!" they said and made themselves scarce.

Then he looked back at us. "William Masterson, McKenzie Killeen, and Tracy Franz?"

I had a bad feeling. Will put an arm around my shoulders. "Yes?" he replied cautiously.

"Makes sense. So, John, have you gotten that thing taken care of yet, or is that why these miscreants are here?" the officer asked.

"It's an ongoing problem. I have every intention of making it right, however," Anders said.

"Good to hear it. Need any help?" the officer continued.

Anders looked at Will. "I think Will could use a ride to Benson, Burlington, and Carver."

"Keeping the girls here as collateral, huh?" the officer grinned.

"It seemed like a smart move." Anders's expression hardened. "Well, Will? What are you waiting for?"

"You know, one of these days, I would love to run into a member of law enforcement who *isn't* corrupt," Will growled. "Just for a change of pace."

The officer laughed. "Good luck with that. All right. Let's get going."

"Will…" I whispered as he peeled himself off me.

He kissed my cheek. "Don't worry, I'll be back." He walked stiffly out of the panic room and began following the officer away. He looked over his shoulder at me and tried to give me an encouraging smile.

I felt sick to my stomach.

"You know most people who mess with these two end up dead, right?" Tracy said to Anders as Will disappeared, her tone threatening.

"I guess we'll see," Anders replied.

11

A PACT WITH SATAN

WILL

I tried not to think of the doors of Benson, Burlington, and Carver as the gates to hell. But the comparison wasn't far from my mind.

They were a large firm on the twenty-eighth floor of the Masterson Building. I tried not to think about the fact that my office was also here. And Ike's.

I was not a bit surprised to see Ike in the law office when Officer Radke pushed me inside.

"Ike," I said tersely by way of greeting.

"Will," Ike replied with a smirk. "John finally nailed you down, I see. I do hope McKenzie and Tracy are okay."

"They're fine," I gritted out.

"Good, good. Of course, it's up to you whether or not they stay that way," he said.

"You don't need to threaten me. John is doing a fine job of that already," I grumbled.

He laughed. "You went for his gold. That man will fart a diamond before he lets anyone touch his gold. You should have known better, Will."

"Clearly." I didn't blame Tracy for trying. It was a good plan that happened to fall apart at the end. I mean, we'd had *actual* mercenaries on our side this time! "Glad you'll finally be able to pay your debts. Seems you've fallen on hard times."

His expression soured. "Yes, well, we can't all go gallivanting around on other people's dimes. I don't think you'll mind having a little of your own spending money, either."

"We'll see." I didn't yet know the terms of the will.

Matt Benson himself, senior partner and founder of the firm, came out to greet us. I'd have liked to say he was an oily, shifty, obvious-piece-of-shit lawyer for the corrupt, but he was actually well-dressed, groomed, and very put together. He had a reassuring smile that crinkled the corners of his eyes and a firm handshake. "Will."

"Matt," I replied.

"I didn't see you at the funeral," he said.

"I was busy with other things," I responded, keeping the niceties going even though it made my chest tight with anger.

"Of course, of course. Well, let's get this show on the road, shall we?" Matt put a hand on my arm and began guiding me gently to his office.

Ike trailed behind.

As soon as his heavy office door was closed and the transparent glass fogged over for privacy, the niceties ended. "You're a hard man to find, Will," Matt said.

"So they tell me," I replied.

He gestured to a chair at a long glass table at the side of his office. "The documents are all laid out. If you need me to explain anything, just ask. Otherwise, the requisite initial and signature places have been tabbed by my secretary."

"I think they call them assistants now," I corrected him, sitting down.

Matt snorted. "'They' might but I don't." He sat down across from me.

Ike sidled in beside me, pulling a chair up close so he could read the documents along with me.

"Grandfather decided not to show you his will?" I needled him.

"He was very specific about no one seeing it until after his death. Not even you, Will," Matt said.

"Probably especially you, you little brat," Ike muttered.

"Careful. I could still decide not to sign it," I grunted.

Ike shrugged. "I'm sure John can teach the girls Russian Roulette with that cannon of his, and we'll see which one comes out alive."

My jaw tensed.

"Ike, please stop saying things like that in front of me. I'd like to be able to claim some semblance of ignorance one of these days," Matt sighed.

"Sorry, Matt. This kid has just been extremely frustrating since the day he was born," Ike said.

"And I'm hoping to be until the day I die," I growled.

Ike gestured to me in a 'see, see?!' motion.

Matt chuckled. "I'm eager to see how you two get on, back in the office together. I think I might just take my coffee upstairs in the mornings and watch. I'm sure it will be quite entertaining."

"Still haven't signed," I reminded them.

"Let's stop bothering him and give him some time to read things over, shall we?" Matt asked.

"Yes. I'd like to read things over myself as well," Ike agreed.

I read pages and pages of the standard inheritance bullshit. I had no trouble initialing and signing that crap. House. Cars. Assets. Blah, blah, blah.

Then, I got to the meat of it. "So… basically what it's saying here is that in order to inherit the business and its assets… I need to continue my relationship with my grandfather's cronies?"

"That's the gist of it, yes," Matt said.

"And if I refuse?" I asked.

Matt shrugged. "The business and its assets will be liquidated. But I'd caution you to think about it. If you refuse to sign and the business is liquidated, the estate will forward evidence of illegal dealings by all of these men to the proper authorities and you will all be prosecuted to the full extent of the law."

"Great, let's do that." I stood. "It's been nice talking to you, gentlemen."

"I believe you missed the important part," Matt said, holding up a hand. "You will be prosecuted as well."

I paused, letting that sink in. Then, I shrugged. "I think, given all the other possible outcomes, that one's not too bad."

"Shame about McKenzie and her family. And Shep and Dolly, of course." Ike examined his fingernails.

"How long do you plan to dangle that one over my head?" I snapped. "It's starting to lose its scare factor. What, are you planning on holding them hostage in little gray boxes for the rest of their lives instead? That's somehow better? Fuck you, Ike."

Ike paled, and it was the best thing I'd seen in a long time. "You can't be serious."

"As a heart attack," I replied flatly. "I'm done. You all can figure the rest of this out. I'll go sit with Officer Radke and wait for my indictment."

"There are, of course, other considerations," Matt said, completely unfazed while Ike began to sweat.

"Really? And what new threat are you laying on the table today?" I scoffed.

Matt reached to the side of the sea of papers and pulled up an untouched envelope. "You won't be the only one going to prison as... collateral damage, I'm afraid. Every child of the organization aged eighteen and over will be implicated. Including your sister."

I stared at him. "Pardon? I don't have a sister. What are you talking about?" Then, I saw red. I grabbed Ike by the collar and shook him like a rag doll. "Did you impregnate Jacey?! She's in her late forties, you sonofabitch!"

"Will, please, let's remain civil. Put Ike down," Matt said calmly. "As far as I know, no new surrogacy attempts have been made."

I dropped Ike back into his chair. He coughed and gasped for air. "What the fuck are you talking about, then?"

Matt pulled the thick packet of papers out of the envelope and handed them to me. "Cora Altier was your egg donor," he summarized while I was reading. "Your grandfather thought she was of good breeding and excellent genetics, so he approached her thirty years ago to donate eggs for… a healthy sum."

I stared at the papers outlining the entire agreement. "Cora… Altier. She wasn't Altier back then."

"No, she wasn't," Matt confirmed.

I swallowed. "She was Cora Franz."

"For seven years. Long enough to have a beautiful, *innocent*, twenty-three-year-old daughter with Morgan Franz," Matt said.

"Tracy," I murmured.

Ike perked up. "I suppose you want her to go to jail, too. Actually, at last count, there were five of you who weren't really involved in anything who would be implicated if and when the evidence was released. I mean, the other four are girls, but then you're living proof that not all men recognize a good thing when they see it. Antonia Fuegos is just turning nineteen, isn't she? McKenzie's age?"

If I ground my teeth any harder, I was going to crack a tooth.

"So young," Ike sighed.

"I swear to God I'm going to kill you if it's the last thing I ever do," I seethed.

"Now, gentlemen, this doesn't have to be contentious," Matt said soothingly. "Will, just sit back down and let's discuss this calmly."

I sank back down into my chair, clutching the papers that revealed the other half of my parentage in my fist. Sister. I had a sister.

And, technically, a mother, but considering how absent she was from Tracy's life, I didn't have high hopes for a relationship there.

Then, there were all those other innocent children of the organization's asshole leaders….

Shit.

"I don't suppose you'll feel as bad about the seven heirs who *are* actually involved in the day-to-day, but I want you to remember that most of them were groomed. Just like you," Matt reminded me.

Bile rose in the back of my throat. "I don't want to be involved in this. In any of this. Can't I just sign this shit over to Ike?"

"That's very sweet, Will. Remind me to get you a rather large wedding present," Ike smiled. "But actually, no. Otherwise, I would have killed you six hundred times by now."

"I'm afraid the will is ironclad. It has to be you," Matt said, actually sounding regretful.

If it was an act, it was a good one. I sighed and started reading the papers again.

"Fuck," I muttered at the end. "Fuck. *Fuck.*" I'd had enough classes in business law to understand most of what I was reading, even if Matt wasn't there to explain it to me. And I did make him explain it to me. Twice.

In the end, when I just stared at the papers before me until they became a blur of legalese, Matt reached into his lapel pocket and handed me his own personal, very heavy pen. "It's for the best, Will," he said.

Ike sat back with a triumphant grin, folding his arms over his chest. "And here I thought I'd have to live in poverty if we couldn't find you. Luckily, you have this wonderful penchant for making new friends, who we can exploit."

I paused, the pen hovering over a signature line. "Matt?"

"Yes?" Matt responded.

"Is there any way to take Ike out of the business altogether?" I asked.

Ike frowned. "Hey! That's not—!"

Matt tapped his fingers on the arms of his chair. "Interesting. Your grandfather did have a betrayal clause."

"Activate it," I said.

"On what grounds?!" Ike spluttered.

"On the grounds that I will never be able to trust you or work with you again," I replied flatly.

Matt nodded slowly. "That makes sense. I'm sure I can figure something out. Legally. He does have quite the golden parachute, however."

"I'll pay," I said. "I don't care. Just as long as he's gone."

"Listen here, you jumped-up little—" Ike began.

I initialed and signed everything with a resigned flourish. "Please have security show Mr. Freeborn out and keep him out while we work on his severance package."

"Of course, Mr. Masterson," Matt smiled.

Ike squawked in protest when two building security guards came in to drag him out. He resisted at first, then shook them off and straightened his jacket. "You're going to regret this, William Masterson the Third."

"Oh, I'm going to regret a lot of things," I responded. "This? Not going to be one of them."

Ike marched out with security.

I turned to Matt. "I suppose there's the matter of my legal fees for all the extra work I'm putting on your plate."

Matt grinned. "Mr. Masterson, you read my mind."

12

TOGETHER AND APART

Tracy and I sat on the edge of Anders's bed, waiting to hear or see any sliver of hope. For me, that was Will coming back. For Tracy?

"My dad is going to sue your ass," Tracy warned Anders. "You won't have a pair of underwear to your name when he's through with you."

"And yet, he knows you're here, and he's not here," he replied in an unbothered tone.

"That's not true," Tracy snapped. "And even if it is, he'll still sue you later."

"Uh-huh." Anders's phone rang. He pulled it from his pocket and put it on speaker. "Morgan, speak of the devil."

"He did it. It's done. Oh, except for the fact he's getting rid of Ike," Franz replied.

"Dad! Dad, I'm here! Mr. Anders has a gun!" Tracy cried.

Franz ignored her. So did Anders.

Anders sighed. "Well, we knew that would happen. Maybe Joel can go over the everyday workings with him instead. He's always been more involved."

"We'll all take a turn, John. It'll be a bit rough in the beginning, I'm sure, but he'll get a feel for it. Will's a smart man," Franz said.

My breath caught. He'd done it. He'd put himself at the head of all of this ugliness.

No doubt he'd done it for me, and for Tracy. And my parents, Shep and Dolly. And probably other people I didn't even know about.

I felt like I was dipped in molasses. Everything felt slow and icky.

"That's it then. I'll shoo the girls out, and you can pick them up and take them wherever. No need to keep pointing a gun at them," Anders said.

"Oh, I don't know. I know at least one who hasn't learned her lesson," Franz grumped.

"Dad!" Tracy protested.

"I think you should stay with Will for a few days," Franz said. "Right now, you're really pissing me off. More than usual."

Tracy frowned. "At least I'm not stealing babies from third world countries!"

"Anders, you are *so* lucky you only had boys," Franz lamented.

"Hey!" She put her hands on her hips even though her father couldn't see it. "I'm right here!"

"It's been much easier with boys, I will admit," Anders said. "I'll get them out to the car."

"Thank you, John." The call ended.

Tracy shot to her feet. "He thinks this conversation is over. He's got another thing coming!"

"It doesn't sound like he's willing to listen to you right now," I said carefully as Anders herded us down the stairs and to the front door.

"Oh, he'll listen." She stomped to the limo and yanked the door open before the chauffeur could open it for her. "Dad—!"

Morgan Franz was nowhere to be seen.

"What, he just sent a car?!" Tracy asked.

Anders started laughing. "That's too good. Well played, Morgan."

She turned to the chauffeur. "I demand to see my father!"

"I'm afraid Mr. Franz has very specific instructions to take you to the Masterson Estate," the chauffeur said apologetically. "If you wouldn't mind just taking your seat, Miss Franz—"

"I want to see my father," she insisted.

"I'm sorry, Miss Franz, but I'm afraid that's not possible," the chauffeur said firmly.

I tugged on her arm. "I don't think that's going to happen today."

"But... ugh, fine." She scooted into the limo. "I want to see Will again, anyway."

"Me too," I said, getting in after her.

The chauffeur closed the door. When he shifted it into drive, he closed the partition between us, clearly opposed to hearing any more argument.

"Asshole," Tracy muttered.

"Who? The driver or your father?" I asked.

"Both." She crossed her arms over her chest. "I hope they didn't force Will to do something awful. Maybe the will wasn't as bad as all of us thought?" she suggested.

I had a very bad feeling. When I met her eyes, I could tell she did, too.

"Maybe your family will be there, at least?" she said quietly, squeezing my knee.

"I hope so," I whispered.

We drove to our old, familiar prison—the Masterson Estate. The wrought-iron gates closed behind us, and I felt immediately trapped.

Tracy took my hand and held it. "Does this place always feel this scary? I don't think I've ever been here before, but... I mean, don't get me wrong, that's pretty." She gestured to the main house coming into view. "But... I mean, damn."

"It's not just you. It always feels this way. It probably has bad energy. Bad things have happened here," I explained.

Will stood at the door of the mansion and I felt relaxed and more tense at the same time. I searched his face as the limo came to a stop, but it was unreadable.

"Not a good sign," she whispered.

"My thoughts exactly." I let go of her hand as the chauffeur opened the door. I got out first, then Tracy.

I walked right to Will and he gathered me into a bone-crushing hug.

"It was bad?" I murmured, stroking his hair.

"It was bad," Will confirmed my suspicions.

"How fucked are you?" Tracy asked, standing right beside us.

"Pretty fucked. But hey, we'll all live in the lap of luxury, and I'm getting Ike ousted, so…."

I shook my head. "This isn't going to break us. We'll still figure this out."

He sighed. "We might have to take a little break for now. Get our feet under us. Get a sense of the situation."

I hugged him tighter. "But you don't want to do any of those things. Why did you agree?"

"Let's just… go inside and talk." He put a hand at my back and gave me a little push.

"Are my parents here? Shep and Dolly?" I asked as we made our way to the living room, Tracy following in our wake.

"I've been assured they will be brought here tonight," he said. He sat me down on the loveseat then sank down next to me.

"Do you mind if I'm here?" Tracy glanced awkwardly at us, then at the armchair beside us.

Will gestured for her to sit. "Please."

She sat and crossed her legs, her body radiating practiced poise while her eyes were nervous. "How did they get you to do it?"

"They used you," he replied without hesitation.

We both stared at him. "What?"

"Not just you. Antonia. The others. Everyone who wasn't actually involved will be implicated if I don't take over. They're going to bury us under a mountain of evidence. Antonia is just days shy of her nineteenth birthday, for God's sake." He closed his eyes. "I couldn't do it. It's one thing to gamble with my future. I almost walked, secure in the knowledge I'd be the only one going down. Then, they dropped the bomb."

"I don't think anyone will seriously believe a nineteen-year-old girl was capable of all the crap our families are involved in. But I see your point." Tracy pursed her lips. "Those assholes."

He bumped his head against mine, clearly tired. "Tracy," he said softly. "Your mother, Cora. Do you see her often?"

"My egg donor? Only when she wants me to attend another one of her weddings."

Will flinched when she said 'egg donor.' "Um...."

"It's all about the optics, you know," she continued with a snort. "I'd refuse to go but Dad insists. Why do you ask? Do you think I should see if I can go stay with her for a while? If something's going down, I want to be a part of it. They're threatening *my* future, too."

"Are you okay, love?" I asked, noticing an odd expression on Will's face.

He swallowed. "Tracy, your mother... really was an egg donor, did you know that?"

"What? Really?" She blinked. "That makes absolutely no sense."

Tracy didn't know what Will was getting at. But, suddenly, I did. "Oh God."

"You remember I was born to a surrogate, right?" he continued.

"Right. Your father... um... died," she said delicately.

"My grandfather paid for an egg donor. Jacey wasn't my biological mother." He swallowed. "It was someone else."

I could see it in her expression when it clicked. "They gave you more than just paperwork to sign. They gave you information on the egg donor. And the egg donor... was my mother."

"Yes," he said. "Yes, it was."

Her hands flew to her mouth. "Oh my God."

"Maybe I should get you both some water," I suggested, beginning to stand.

Will pulled me back down next to him. "Please, don't go."

"But—"

"You're my brother," she gasped. "Oh my God."

"Really, water would be a good thing right now," I tried to convince him.

He kissed my temple. "Please. Just for a little bit. Stay."

"What's water going to do? We need… I don't know. I don't know how to feel about it. I don't know if we need scotch or champagne." Tracy laughed nervously.

Will let out a loud laugh. "Same for me. But… I think we're both good people, so I'm leaning toward champagne."

"This is better than a gender reveal. Do we call it an 'egg reveal'?" she chuckled.

I just glanced back and forth between the two of them. "I suppose I could find some streamers?"

That just made them laugh harder. I finally joined in, deciding no one was going to faint or get hysterical at that point.

"Champagne. Though we should probably have something to eat first," Will decided. "We've all had kind of a long, food-free day."

A woman discreetly shuffled up to us then, and I jumped. "Who —?"

"I hired a new housekeeper," he explained. "In fact, I've turned over all the staff. I don't want anything or anyone associated with Ike here. Tomorrow, a security firm is coming to remove most of the cameras."

"How many cameras do you have?" Tracy asked.

"More than you want to know. I'm just hoping the security personnel can find them all," he sighed. He turned and grinned at the housekeeper. "Ladies, this is Camille. Camille, meet McKenzie and Tracy. McKenzie is my fiancée."

"I'm pleased to meet you." Camille gave us a nice smile and had a warm energy about her. I was glad the last housekeeper had been replaced. "I couldn't help but hear you three might be hungry?"

"Starving," Tracy groaned. "He *had* to mention it. I wasn't hungry before, but now I'm famished."

Camille chuckled. "Dear me. I'll have to fix you something. Are sandwiches all right? I'll make a variety."

"That's wonderful. Thank you, Camille," he said.

"I'll also bring some water. And champagne." She winked at us before walking away.

Yes, I definitely liked her better. "So, you've been making some changes," I said.

"As many as I can," Will replied. "I at least want control over my home environment. Speaking of which, Tracy, you can stay as long as you need to. Or, even, just as long as you like. I'm getting the impression from Morgan that he's not very happy with you right now."

"Well, I'm not very happy with him, so I guess we're even," Tracy sniffed. "He can't keep me from going home. What's he going to do? Have my bodyguard throw me out?"

He winced. "Still...."

"I'll stay here tonight. We'll see how things look in the morning." Now she looked tired.

"I think after sandwiches and champagne, maybe we ought to go take a nap," I suggested. "What time are the others getting here, Will? Do you know?"

"I'm not sure," he admitted. "They just said 'evening.' I tried pushing but... well, anyway, I told them they'd get paid when our family and friends got here. I'm hoping that's enough of an incentive to get them here sooner."

"Money always makes things happen sooner. Who knows? Maybe they'll be back by the time we finish the champagne?" Tracy said.

"I hope so," I responded.

13

DAMAGED DELIVERY

Will

They were not back by the time we finished the champagne.

As the sun faded and night crept in, and with it nerve-wracking darkness, Tracy, McKenzie, and I sat in the living room waiting. And waiting.

We'd fallen silent at dusk. By eleven-fifty, Tracy was tapping her fingers on the arm of her chair and McKenzie had a bruising grip on my hand.

"You're sure they're coming today? Because in ten minutes, it's going to be tomorrow," Tracy finally said, glancing down at the phone beside her.

"Can you try calling them again?" McKenzie asked. She was tired. We all were. We were all also determined to be present when our four friends/family arrived.

"I can try again." I didn't know what good it was going to do. They hadn't answered my last five calls. I figured if they wanted more money or something, they would have at least answered. What was wrong?

I went to my recent calls and was just about to tap the anonymous number there, when it actually blinked on the screen, indicating they were calling me.

"This is Will Masterson," I said, answering quickly. I put them on speaker.

"We're here. Be ready to wire the money," a voice replied gruffly.

"Of course. I'm on my way." I got up and tried to let go of McKenzie's hand, but she was having none of it.

"I'm coming, too," she insisted.

"Me, too," Tracy said.

I didn't know if we had a lot of time, so I just gave in with a sigh. I wasn't going to win that argument, anyway, no matter how long we stood there. I led them to the front door. Camille had gone home for the day, which I was thankful for once I opened the door myself.

Four loved ones, looking very much worse for the wear, knelt between a group of thugs. One mercenary approached me, stone-faced and indifferent. He pointed at my phone. "Money."

"Yes, of course." I stood close to him so I could get the wire transfer details.

"What the actual fuck?!" Tracy gaped, looking at our four returning group members. "What the fuck did you do to them?!"

"Tracy, these people don't care. We have to just go through the motions and get them back," McKenzie whispered loud enough for me to hear.

"Yes, but, just… I mean… *look* at them!" Tracy pointed.

I was trying very hard not to look at them, but Tracy stabbing a finger in their direction made me look up.

Dolly and Jacey both had bruises all over, especially on their faces. They wore old, ill-fitting clothes, which made me suspect something had happened to their old ones. I didn't want to imagine what or why.

Caleb and Shep were also pretty banged up. Caleb was oozing blood through his shirt in front and in back, while the gentle giant of a trucker was shirtless and bleeding from busted stitches in his abdomen.

My eye twitched. "I don't suppose you could have brought them here in any better shape?" I asked blandly.

"Just be glad you got them at all. We were going to kill them the day after you called us back," the mercenary said. "Freeborn didn't pay his debts and told us to do what we wanted with them."

Ike is a dead man. I'd clipped his wings, but he deserved more. So much more. "Well, I do pay my debts." I finished authorizing the wire transfer.

We both watched as the money transferred from one of my Cayman Islands accounts to theirs. No need for the FBI or CIA to get involved in our business by using American accounts. It was already a risk that they'd be watching all this activity. But, after everything that had happened these last few months, I could say with absolute confidence that the FBI could go fuck itself.

Once the transfer was complete, the mercenary nodded. "Time to drop off the packages, boys. We've got the money."

The thugs turned and walked away from Caleb, Shep, Jacey, and Dolly, leaving them swaying in the middle of my driveway. While the mercenaries got in their trucks and drove away, we ran to our four missing members.

"Dad!" McKenzie said, kneeling next to Caleb and catching him against her shoulder just as he would have fallen over.

Tracy rightly ascertained the next most damaged person was Shep. She stripped his shirt off of him and crouched down, pressing his wadded shirt to the busted stitches. "Don't worry. I'll call our doctor. He makes house calls." She looked around. "I'll... tell him to bring his whole team."

"Thanks, Tracy. I'm not sure I want my doctor here, but if your doctor needs the back-up, I'll call him. I just don't know if he's working for Ike," I explained, carefully helping Dolly, then Jacey to their feet and then letting them lean on me.

While Tracy called her doctor, Jacey gripped my arm. "Is McKenzie okay?" she asked anxiously.

"She's fine. We're just worried about all of you," I reassured her. "How are you two doing?"

Dolly and Jacey looked at each other. "We've been better," Dolly quipped.

"I figured. I'm going to bring you two in the house, all right? I'll get you sitting down in the living room. Maybe we need to get Caleb and Shep back into beds," I murmured. "At least until the doctor gets here."

"Please take good care of them," Jacey said. "They're in such awful shape."

"I'm surprised they could get Caleb to kneel. Now I just have to figure out how we're going to get him back up," I sighed.

Someone in the dark cleared their throat, and I jumped.

"Sorry, sir." It was one of the new guards I'd hired, one of the three stationed at the gate. "We couldn't help but notice your predicament, so Charlie and I called Isaac and Peter to fill our spots at the security office and came right over. We need to get the men inside?"

Garret. His name was Garret. "Yes, Garret. Thank you. If you could help, that would be greatly appreciated," I said.

"It'll be our pleasure, sir. We were a little worried when you told us to let those mercenaries in. We could tell they were serious people. Then we could see they weren't doing real well when they dropped these four on the ground, so we figured we should come help." Garret moved behind Caleb. "Just fall backward if you can, sir. Don't worry, Miss Kent. We're gonna take good care of him."

Caleb took his hand away from McKenzie, then patted her cheek. "It's all going to be okay." He slumped backward, and Garret caught him.

Charlie took his legs and they carefully lifted him and started into the house.

"Go, I'll get your mom and Dolly after they come back for Shep," I said to McKenzie.

She nodded and ran after her father.

"Thanks for looking after my Shep, honey," Dolly told Tracy, sounding fatigued. "You're all good kids. I don't regret a thing."

I had a bad feeling. "Dolly? How-how are you feeling?"

"Better." She smiled. "Better, now."

Tracy got her phone out again, her hand shaking. "Hello? Doctor

O'Leary? I'm going to need you to get here as quickly as possible. And maybe keep an ambulance on standby."

"It's too dangerous. I've been screwing people over left and right, and I'm going to be screwing over more, and they know it," I said. "We can't take them to a regular hospital."

"Life and death, Will. Life and death," Tracy snapped.

Dolly slid off my arm and tumbled to the ground.

"Ma!" Shep wheezed, pushing Tracy aside to try to get to her.

"No, Mr. Shep!" she protested. "Your stitches!"

He leaned over his mother. "Ma, can you hear me?"

Dolly didn't answer.

"Ma. Ma!" He gave her a little shake.

"Do something, Will," Jacey said, giving me a gentle push. "I'm fine. I'll just sit down until the doctor gets here or the guards take me inside."

I didn't know what to do. I had no idea what to do. "Garret! Charlie!" I yelled.

The two men came running out. "We just got him settled, sir. We —Lord have mercy." Garret knelt on the other side of Dolly as I scooted out of the way. "Okay. Okay, we've got a situation." He pressed his fingers to her neck. "Shit. Pulse is hardly there at all. Charlie, call them down at the security office and tell them to bring up the defibrillator."

Charlie talked quickly into his shoulder walkie-talkie while Shep turned pale. I hoped it was from emotion and not from blood loss.

"Take Jacey into the house, please, Tracy, if you can," I said, recognizing this was something I should probably shield her from. There was no need for my sister to become as jaded and used to violence as McKenzie and I were.

"But—" Tracy argued.

"Please," I reiterated, staring her right in the eyes.

Tracy sighed and went over to Jacey. "Can you stand?" she asked.

"I don't know," Jacey replied, trying with Tracy's help.

Charlie caught Jacey when she began to fall. "I'll carry her, Miss Franz. You just walk in with us. I'm sure with Mr. Kent down and being looked after by Miss Kent, Mrs. Kent could use someone watching over her as well."

"Well...." Tracy finally gave in with a sigh. "All right."

Charlie lifted Jacey up in his arms and, when Tracy wasn't looking, he winked at me.

I could have kissed him.

The two went into the house while Garret kept checking Dolly's pulse and Shep watched over his mother.

Just as another guard—Eric—got there with the defibrillator, Garret swore. "You got that thing fired up?"

"Yeah, I do," Eric said.

"Good. Because I'm about to do CPR, and I want that thing ready." Garret got to work.

I couldn't breathe. Shep made choking noises, staying out of the way, but never leaving his mother's side. I knew I had nothing on Shep, and that I'd only known her a few short months, but it wasn't hard for me to realize Dolly was the closest thing to a mother I'd ever experienced my whole life.

"I can't get a pulse," Garret said, tensely. "Let's get the leads attached."

As they ripped open her shirt, revealing more black bruising, my heart broke.

Suddenly, Shep grabbed me by my shirt and brought me down to his level. His face was contorted with rage.

I expected him to scream at me, or even hit me. I deserved it. I should never have brought either of them into this mess. "I'm sorry," I whispered. "I'm so sorry."

"Will," he seethed.

"Clear!" Garret called.

Dolly gave no response.

"Yes?" I said to Shep.

"I ain't mad at you," he continued.

That threw me. "You should be."

"Again, Eric!" Garret ordered. "Clear!"

No response from Dolly.

Shep looked over at his mother, his expression melting into sadness, then turned back to me.

"Me and ma, we wanted to help you. But there's a whole buttload of jackasses you need to deal with," he told me.

I wasn't sure what to say to that. "I... wish I had some of them here."

"Again!" Garret said.

"Yeah, me, too," Shep replied. "Then I could kill them with my bare hands." He shook his head. "If Ma's really gone, then you got work to do."

"We don't know that yet. And the doctor is coming." I didn't want to give him false hope, but I didn't think yet that there was none.

Shep gripped my shirt tighter as Dolly continued to lay on the ground without a pulse, Garret and Eric still working hard to bring her around. "Will, I ain't rich, and I don't know a lot about what all you got going on with your grandfather's mess. But I do know one thing I want you to do for me if Ma dies."

"Anything, Shep. But like I said, the doctor—" I began.

Garret looked at me and slowly shook his head, even while he and Eric kept going. "The doctor's here," he said softly as a sleek silver BMW came rolling up, followed by no less than four other cars.

The doctor leapt out of his car and ran to Dolly, briefly watching the guards' progress before jumping in himself.

His team surrounded her and it was impossible to see. But we could hear them talking amongst themselves. It didn't sound good.

"Will," Shep rumbled, getting my attention once more.

"Time of death twelve-twenty-eight AM," Dr. O'Leary sighed in frustration.

Shep's eyes welled up, but his expression went dangerously dark. "Will."

"Shep, I'm so—" I choked out.

"I want you to burn it all down," he growled. "Every last goddamn one of them."

14

EVERYONE FALLS APART

MᴄKᴇɴᴢɪᴇ

Dad was laying down on the sofa in the living room. The nice guard named Charlie had carried in Mom, and she was sitting in a chair right next to the sofa. Tracy and I had both tried to insist that she lay down, but she'd been adamant.

Stubborn woman.

I wondered why I hadn't seen Garret yet, or Shep, Will, or Dolly. In fact, Charlie was standing sentinel, suspiciously close to the hallway, as though he was ready to block us if we tried to go back.

A bad feeling curled into the pit of my stomach.

Then, who I could only presume was Dr. O'Leary came striding into the living room, a passel of people behind him. Inside what must have been twelve support personnel was Garret and another guard shouldering Shep between them. He looked truly awful.

Will came after all of them, holding his phone to his ear. "Yes, Camille. I hate to bother you at this time of night, but I'm going to need someone to come hold down the fort. If you could rouse some of the other staff, that would be greatly appreciated. People who aren't bothered by the sight of blood."

I looked around as the assistants parted. *No Dolly?*

"Where's the nice older lady?" Tracy asked, echoing my thoughts. There was a long silence.

"She's being taken to the hospital, lovey," Dr. O'Leary said absently. He assessed the room and his gaze zeroed in on Dad. "Him first."

Four assistants swarmed over. Then, the doctor. "Excuse us, young lady. We need to get to work now."

"Oh, of course. I'll get out of the way," I said, going over to Mom.

"What's his name?" Dr. O'Leary asked while one of his team came over to examine Mom.

"Caleb. Caleb Kent," I replied quickly. The doctor seemed to be the kind that wanted his answers immediately.

"Caleb, I have an imaging machine on its way, but I'm going to take a look at you while I have you here. You're bleeding in several places, and I don't like it," the doctor said. He looked at me again. "Quick medical history."

"He was just fine until recently. In the last few months, he's been in a bomb explosion and gotten shot in the chest, just shy of his heart. We lead… interesting lives now," I explained.

Dr. O'Leary snorted. "You're associated with a Masterson. It's to be expected." His eyes flicked to Tracy. "The nice older lady is dead," he said, too quietly for Tracy to hear.

I froze. So did Mom. "What?" I wheezed.

"I don't know what an autopsy would find, but I am speculating that her wounds were too severe and put too much strain on her heart. I'm sorry," he added.

Tears stung my eyes, and my chest felt like an iron band had been tightened around it. "Oh my God, Shep…."

"I would rather Tracy not know. It might be impossible to keep it from her, but I'd like to try," Dr. O'Leary said. "She… shouldn't be mixed up in whatever this is. I've called her father to send a car for her."

I glanced at Tracy, who had stationed herself next to Shep. "Probably for the best. But… um… Shep is Dolly's son. He might…."

"I've already asked him to keep it quiet until Tracy is gone. He agrees that whomever can be spared from this situation, should be." The doctor went back to examining Dad.

Will finished on the phone and went to sit on the other side of Shep. He looked at me, and I nodded. It was the right place for him to be right now.

Mom was quiet, but took my hand, hers shaking.

"Dolly was a really good person, Mom," I whispered.

She nodded her agreement. I don't think she trusted herself to speak.

"I think he's good to be moved to a bed. Does he have a room here?" Dr. O'Leary asked.

"Yes. I don't know if it's made up, but I'll go see." I tried to let go of Mom's hand, but her grip was firm.

"Don't leave me," she begged.

That surprised me. "No, Mom. O-of course not! Will?" I called. "Can you check and see if Mom and Dad's room is ready?"

"Not a problem." He stood and strode quickly down the hall.

"So it's on the main floor. Excellent," Dr. O'Leary said.

Will trotted back quickly. "It's all made up. I turned down the bed to make things easier."

"Good. You there, strapping young security guards! I need this man moved—carefully—to a bedroom. Please lead the way, Mr. Masterson," the doctor stated.

"You don't have a gurney?" Will asked.

"It's on its way, along with a portable CT scanner, X-ray, and ultrasound. The equipment truck couldn't get here as fast as we could," Dr. O'Leary explained.

Garret and Charlie picked up my father and, with great care, carried him down the hall, Will leading the way.

"We should go with them, Mom," I murmured, putting my other hand over her wrist. "Can you walk?"

"I don't know." Mom hiccuped, tears beginning to stream down her cheeks. "Oh God, I don't know anything anymore."

A lump formed in my throat. "Mom... um... are you having some kind of breakdown?"

"I don't know!" she wailed.

Tracy put a hand on Shep's shoulder, and he dismissed her with a nod. She came over to Mom and me. "Hey, Mrs. Kent? Is everything okay?"

"No!" Mom shouted. "Nothing is okay! Nothing! I'm so sick of this! Everybody dies! Everybody!"

Oh no. "Um, Tracy? Maybe you should go back over by Shep...."

"No, I'm fine right here," she said firmly.

"I really think—" I tried again.

Mom speared Tracy with a wild look. "And you're going to die, too!"

"*Mom!!!*" I put a hand over her mouth. "She doesn't mean it. She's just been under a lot of stress."

Tracy took a deep breath. "That nice older woman. She's dead, isn't she?"

"Um..." I cast around for something to say. I didn't want to lie to her, but I didn't want to scare her, either. The doctor and Shep were right. She shouldn't be involved if she didn't have to be.

"You don't have to say anything," she said. "I can see it on your face. And hers. And his." She indicated Mom and Shep in turn.

"It was just too much for her heart," I tried to explain gently.

Tracy swallowed. "They were all tortured."

Mom snorted behind my hand, and I knew she had a comment on that, just as I knew I probably shouldn't let her voice it.

"Look. Dr. O'Leary contacted your dad. He's sending a car for you. When it gets here, you need to leave. You can't be here. It's just gotten way too real, and I don't want you to get hurt. I don't think you're in deep enough yet that you can't get out," I said.

Tracy frowned at me. "I'm in. I'm in all the way."

"But—"

Tracy pulled out her phone. "Dad? You can cancel the car. I'm staying at the Masterson Estate for the foreseeable future."

"No, don't! It's dangerous! Tracy, you don't understand what you're doing!" I cried.

"Yes, I mean it. I won't get in the car when it gets here, so you might as well cancel it. Yes, that was McKenzie. You know what? She probably is right. But I'm not leaving my brother and sister-in-law to be," she said flatly.

My throat went dry. "Tracy…."

"Yes, I know. Well, apparently the lawyer told Will, and then Will told me. You knew? Gee, thanks for letting me know." Her tone was scathing as she spoke to her father. "My own protection? You know what, I'm tired of this whole 'for my own protection' bullshit. What's so special about me that *I* need protecting? Why not try protecting these poor tortured people who just showed up on Will's doorstep? Hm? Did you know about them? Did you, Dad?!"

I sighed and leaned my head on Mom's shoulder. *Tracy, you stubborn fool.*

Tracy ended the call abruptly. "He wouldn't answer my question, so that's a yes."

"I'm sure they all knew, Tracy. But that doesn't mean you want to antagonize any of them, including your father," I said.

"They deserve to be antagonized. Look what they did!" She gestured around her.

"I know. But they're also very dangerous, and you could get hurt," I pointed out.

"You all have already gotten hurt. If I can help, I want to. It's important to me. And you're not going to convince me to go away," she said.

I groaned. "Fine. Just don't say I didn't warn you." I waved one of the doctor's assistants, who had been standing patiently by, over to Mom. "I think you've seen that my mother is either overly tired or having a nervous collapse. Help?" I cautiously pulled my hand away from Mom's mouth.

Mom had calmed down some. At least, I hoped that was the case.

My hope shattered, however, when she grabbed the assistant's wrist and whispered, "We're all going to die."

"Fuck."

I looked up and saw Will. I suddenly felt a nervous breakdown coming on myself.

As though sensing it, he came around the sofa and put an arm around me. "It'll be okay, honeybee. Dr. O'Leary is very proficient. I'm sure once your dad is feeling better, Jacey will, too."

Tracy must have decided I was okay with Will there and went back to Shep.

I wanted to say something to Will, to Mom, just to make the situation better somehow. But I didn't know the words. I kept wracking my brain as equipment began rolling into the mansion and Dr. O'Leary's assistants began setting it up.

Camille and staff arrived shortly thereafter. Nice as she was, she commanded them like a drill sergeant and had sandwiches, fruit, salads, and beverages ready in no time.

Then, Shep was moved to his bedroom to be examined and treated by the doctor. Tracy went along.

All the activity made my head spin.

It was dawn before Dr. O'Leary finally got to Mom. "I hear you're not feeling very well," he said to her kindly.

Mom shook in her chair. "Everyone dies."

"Yes. When it's their time. But I think you've still got a long run ahead of you," he assured her.

Mom burst into tears. "No. No, I don't. I know I don't. Masterson, he kills everything he touches!"

"Well, then it's a good thing he's dead, now isn't it?" Dr. O'Leary said.

"It doesn't matter. It's like his ghost is everywhere," Mom hissed.

He patted Mom's hand. "I think you'd like to go sit with your husband. He's doing very well. But if you want to sit with him, you have to pull it together. Do you understand?"

Mom was quiet for a moment. Then, she took a deep breath. "I think I can do that."

"Good. Because we don't want to go scaring Caleb, now do we?" he asked.

"No. No, I won't," Mom answered. "I'm sorry."

"That's okay. Everyone falls apart at some time or another. Julia? I want you to get some Ativan for Jacey here. I think she just needs to calm down a little bit." He turned to Mom. "It's just some tiny pills. It will help."

"Okay," Mom whispered.

I sagged against Will, feeling so relieved I could have fainted. "Thank you, doctor."

"Like I said, everyone falls apart sometimes." He patted Mom's hand again, then stood. "Why don't you come with me? I'll get you settled."

"I'd like that." Mom got up and went with the doctor.

I waited until she was out of sight, then started to cry.

Will held me in his arms and kissed away my tears. "Let's go to bed, love. It's been a long couple of days."

I nodded and began staggering toward our bedroom, feeling heavy and lightheaded at the same time.

He swooped me up in his arms. "We'll be better equipped to face all this after a nice, long rest."

I hoped he was right.

15

FINDING A WAY

WILL

I wrapped my arms around McKenzie as we laid in our bed. We'd both changed clothes, her for a nude nighty from the closet and me into a pair of black silk boxers. We were exhausted.

Still, she wasn't sleeping. I could always tell the difference.

"You should get some sleep," I said softly.

"I can't sleep. My parents are in pain and Shep… God only knows how Shep is doing," she replied.

I swept her honey-colored hair aside and kissed the back of her neck. "We've got a full medical team here. Hopefully, everyone's going to be okay from here on out."

"Except for Dolly," she whispered.

I swallowed a lump in my throat. "Except for Dolly."

"She was a good person. She didn't deserve that," she said.

"She didn't. But she did say she didn't regret helping us," I told her.

McKenzie turned in my arms. "When?"

"Just before she died. And no, I'm not making that up for your sake," I said.

She went quiet. Then, she started to cry.

I pulled her against my body, cradling her head against my shoulder. "I'm so sorry, honeybee."

"I'm sorry. Don't tell the doctor. I'm really not falling apart like Mom," she begged.

"Of course not. Jesus, you're allowed to have emotions," I reassured her.

McKenzie cried harder. "This is all so awful. And now they've gotten you to sign the contract with Satan, so it's like it was all for nothing!"

So that was the foot of it. *Crap.* "You know I'm going to use my position whatever way I have to, to bring it all down, right?"

"I know you're going to try," she said bitterly. "But I know what your grandfather was like."

I set her back a bit, grabbing her by the shoulders. "Look at me."

She raised her wet eyes to mine.

"I am going to *end* this. I don't care what I have to do or what it's going to cost. When I am finished, there will be nothing left but you, and me, and our family. And you will go to school. Then, we'll get married. We'll have kids, and your parents will be grandparents, and my sister will be an auntie, and everyone will be *blissfully* happy for the rest of eternity. That's just how it's going to be. Do you understand me?" I stated.

McKenzie nodded. "Okay."

"Okay," I repeated. I pulled her against me again. "I'm going to need to go into the office tomorrow and get the lay of the land. I want you to stay here and hold down the fort while I'm gone."

"Okay," she said again.

I looked down at her. "And don't just agree with me because you think it's the answer I want to hear. I want to know your real thoughts."

"Okay." She bit her lip.

"So, what are you thinking?" I prodded.

"I'm... um... thinking that if you have to go to work tomorrow and neither of us is getting any sleep anyway..." she said slowly.

My dick immediately perked up. "Yes?" I purred.

"That maybe we should play cards?" she grinned.

I snorted. "Not unless it's strip poker."

"I've always wanted to play that," she teased.

I stroked a hand down over her breast. "Do you really want to learn now?"

She shivered. "No."

"I didn't think so." I kept sliding my hand down, smoothing it over her ass, then deeper between her legs to finger her through her panties.

My honeybee was already wet for me.

McKenzie moaned and ground against my hand.

I pulled my hand back and licked my fingers.

"Mean!" she protested.

"You know it," I grinned.

She smiled back, then grabbed me by the dick.

"Eep," I gulped. "Gentle, honeybee."

"I know what I'm doing." She slid her hand slowly up my shaft through my boxers, then dipped her hand under my waistband and touched me for real.

"You win!" I said, clutching her wrist. "I know. I was bad. I'm sorry."

"You should be. Starting to get me all worked up and then just pulling back," she sniffed. "Although… maybe I should give you a little attention first."

I swallowed. "I won't say no to that offer."

"Or, maybe we should give each other attention at the same time," she winked.

My cock liked that idea very much and wasn't shy about letting her know.

McKenzie giggled. "Okay. Let's do this."

I shimmied out of my boxers and peeled her panties off.

"No ripping today?" she teased.

"Well, if I did it every time, it wouldn't be a surprise," I said. "Now, if you don't mind, I'd like some of that honey."

Her expression turned sultry. I laid on my back and she clambered over me, sticking her dripping entrance right in my face.

McKenzie's mouth was now directly over my dick.

I pulled her hips back and stuck my tongue right in the honeycomb.

She gasped, her silk nightie rubbing deliciously against my skin as she squirmed on top of me.

I pinched her ass after a while, reminding her she also had a job to do.

Shivering, she wrapped her hand around the base of my straining cock and licked the trickle of precum off my shaft.

Then, she fisted my cock from base to tip, giving me little licks in between.

It was maddening.

The name of the game seemed to be 'who can keep it up the longest.' And I was determined to win.

I swirled my tongue inside her, sucked on her clit, and even teased her with my fingers. She gave me plenty of honey in return, which I happily swallowed.

McKenzie took the head of my cock in her mouth and sucked, still jerking me off.

I wanted to come. I wanted to come so badly. But I also wanted to win.

I pinched her clit as she began to take me down her throat.

It was a mistake. She jumped and accidentally bit me.

"Fuck," I said with a wince, pulling back a bit.

She looked back at me with an apologetic expression on her face. "Sorry."

I smacked her ass. "What are you going to do to make it up to me?"

McKenzie gave me a slow, sexy smile, and I knew I was in for it. She climbed off my chest, depriving me of my access to the promised land, took a firm hold of the base of my dick, and began deep-throating me.

"Not fair..." I wheezed, reaching for her. But she wriggled her hips away.

This was the most fantastic head she'd ever given me. *After I come, I'm going to owe her a puppy. Or maybe a yacht.*

Then all conscious thought faded and all I could do was moan. I tangled my fingers in her hair, panting.

I kept enough wits about me not to shove her down on my cock, though. I'd learned that lesson the hard way and didn't want her to stop.

My balls tightened and very soon I was emptying my cum down her throat.

She gulped, then licked her lips. She patted my still semi-hard dick. "Good boy."

Something snapped inside my brain and I pounced on her, rolling her underneath me while she shrieked with laughter.

"Somebody's very needy today," she gasped as I pushed inside her.

I gently bit her neck. "I don't think that's a complaint."

"Hell no! I'm needy, too." She looped her arms around my neck and arched into me as I started to thrust.

McKenzie was warm, wet, and tight as usual. It didn't take long for me to go from semi-hard to fully erect and desperate for release. "How can you always be so tight?" I groaned.

"It's your f-fault for being so b-big," she chattered, moving her body with mine.

The world exploded behind my eyes and all there was, was white-hot pleasure. She came that same moment, and I felt her nails drag down my back while I sank my teeth into her shoulder.

We collapsed together. I tried, with great effort, to get off of her so I didn't crush her, but she clung to me so the best I could do was hold her and roll us both to the side.

"Don't take it out," she panted, resting her head tiredly on my arm.

I nodded and cupped her ass, holding myself inside her. "You okay, honeybee?"

"Let's go again," she said.

"Sure," I replied. "I was planning to. After we rested a bit."

She grabbed my face. "No. It has to be now!"

I frowned. "Honeybee, you haven't even caught your breath! And male biology doesn't quite work that way…."

"I don't care. We can do it! We love each other," she said desperately.

I wrapped my arms around her more tightly. "Of course we love each other. But it just isn't possible right now. Give me fifteen, maybe thirty minutes. Forty-five at the outside."

"We can't stop," she whimpered.

I gave her a soft kiss. "What's wrong, honeybee?"

"Everything." She sniffled. "Just… just make it go away, Will, please!"

My heart broke for her. "Okay. But I'll have to take it out."

McKenzie sighed and nodded. "Okay."

I kissed her again, then gently pulled out.

A tear rolled down her cheek.

"It's okay, honeybee. I'm still here." I threaded my fingers through hers, then rolled her underneath me again.

She spread her legs.

"I'm getting there," I promised. I nibbled and sucked my way down her body, tasting her salty-sweet skin.

McKenzie arched her back, her free hand digging into my hair, pushing me down where she wanted me.

If this wasn't a mission of mercy, I might have been a little annoyed. But this was about giving her what she needed, so I stopped sampling and focused on the main course. I dipped my tongue inside her.

"Yesss," she sighed, rubbing herself against my face. "Yes, please, Will!"

I could taste both her and myself and I didn't mind one bit. I settled between her thighs, determined to be there for the long haul, still holding one of her hands.

She shuddered and moaned, bucking her hips underneath me.

God, she tasted incredible. At this rate, I was going to be ready in less than fifteen minutes.

McKenzie came against my mouth with a scream.

I lapped up her juices, then kissed the inside of her thigh. "Was that good, honeybee?"

She nodded vigorously. "More."

Shit. "You need a break, love. I do, too. Just a little one." I tried to reason with her.

McKenzie pushed insistently on my head. "I don't want to think anymore. I don't want to think ever again!"

Worry twisted in my gut. *Shit. SHIT.* "Honeybee...."

"JUST DO YOUR FUCKING JOB!!!" she yelled.

My head snapped up, dislodging her hand. "Excuse me?!"

She put her hand over her mouth. "Oh my God."

"He's not going to save you from this one," I grouched. I crawled up the bed and sat down next to her with my arms crossed.

"I didn't mean it. I'm sorry. I'm so sorry," she gasped.

"McKenzie," I said sternly. "I realize you're really going through it right now, and I'm trying to be understanding, because you know I know how that feels. But I'm not your sex slave."

She teared up. "I know. I'm sorry."

"I mean, we can play that out sometime if you want, but we'd have to talk about boundaries and safe words and things like that." I smiled slightly, trying to soften the blow.

It didn't work. She just looked more miserable. "I don't want you to be my sex slave. I just want you to be Will."

"That's a relief. I just want you to be my honeybee." I stroked her hair. "I love you, McKenzie. That's not ever going to change. And I know you've had a really rough night. But that... hurt."

"I'm sorry," she said again. Tears streamed down her cheeks. "Will, I'm so scared."

I snuggled down next to her and took her in my arms. "I know. But your mother's a strong woman. She'll get through whatever breakdown she's experiencing."

"No. I'm scared about you." She took a shaky breath. "What happens tomorrow?"

"What do you mean?" I asked, confused. "I'm going into the office. I told you."

McKenzie wrapped her arms around me, holding me tight. "I'm afraid they'll make you into something you're not."

My heart sank. I kissed her hair. "That won't happen."

"How? How can you guarantee that?" she whispered.

I rubbed her back. "You're going to guarantee it, of course."

"What? How?" She looked up at me.

"I'm coming home to you every night. I know if I'm ever going to deserve you, I *have* to be a good man," I told her.

She sniffled. "That's true."

"So, I wouldn't worry too much about it," I soothed. "As long as I have you, everything is going to be fine."

16

HOLDING DOWN THE FORT

McKenzie

I did worry.

When Will kissed me after two hours of sleep and sat up in bed, I worried.

When he got up and showered, I worried.

When he put on an Armani suit, Rolex, and expensive shoes, I worried.

I could feel he had his armor on and was ready to go into battle.

I was just afraid the dragon was too big for one man.

"Do you have to go?" I asked, catching his arm after he finished putting on his shoes.

He gave me a wan smile and kissed me. "It's all going to be okay, honeybee."

I couldn't stop the whimper of doubt that escaped my throat.

"Remember, I promised to make it okay. And I'm going to," he said gently. "I *have* to go in. So, I need you to hold down the fort here. We've got a lot going on here."

I nodded. "I know."

"Think you can handle it?" he asked.

With a swallow, I nodded again. "I can handle it."

"There's my good girl." He kissed my forehead, then my mouth. Then, he stood. "I love you. I'll be home before you know it."

"I love you, too," I replied, forcing an encouraging smile.

Will chuckled. "Nice try, but the 'I love you' was sincere. Don't worry. You're not alone. I'm going to be thinking about you all day, too."

I smiled for real this time.

"I'll see you tonight." He kissed me again and walked out the door.

I sat for a few minutes, wallowing and worrying. Then, I got up and went to shower myself. Everyone else would be awake soon, and like Will said, we had a lot going on here at home.

By the time I left our suite, Camille was halfway through preparing breakfast with two other staff. There was fruit, pancakes, waffles, French toast… just about a whole diner menu and then some.

"I'm… not sure everyone will be awake at the same time," I said apologetically, stepping in to help.

Camille chased me out of the kitchen. "Of course not. That's what the chafing dishes are for. Sit down in the dining room. We'll bring you something to eat."

"But—"

"Go sit," she repeated in a tone that brooked no argument.

I gave up. I went and sat in the dining room, alone at a giant, long table.

I wasn't alone for long. Just as one of the staff—Krissy—came to take my order, Tracy came in and sat down. She looked wrecked.

"How's Shep?" I asked.

"He finally got to sleep." She waited for Krissy to finish writing down my breakfast order, then rattled off a few things herself. "Do you know where she was taken? He wants to arrange services."

"Here in Minnesota?" I asked.

Tracy nodded. "They're originally from here. He wants to lay her to rest with her parents in Minneapolis. Apparently, they're in a nice cemetery near Lake Harriet."

"I'll find out where she is and have someone come talk to Shep about funeral arrangements," I said. "I'm... just so sorry this happened."

"Me, too."

I would have said more, but breakfast was rushed out in front of us, steaming hot and smelling delicious.

Tracy and I dug right in and there was no talking for a good fifteen minutes.

When I looked up from my plate, my mother was standing in the doorway.

"Mom!" I managed around a mouthful of waffle.

"Hi darling." She looked absolutely wrecked. "I thought I'd come see how you were doing and get some breakfast for your father."

I swallowed my waffle. "Everything is going just fine. Nothing to worry about. You should sit down and eat something before you get back to Dad. I'll go sit with him."

Mom gazed longingly at my waffles. "I really shouldn't. He needs me."

"You'll be a lot more use to him if you don't pass out," Tracy pointed out, cutting another wedge of her omelet.

"True," Mom conceded. She sighed in defeat and sat down.

Krissy was there at her elbow immediately. "What can I get for you, Mrs. Kent?"

Mom bit her lip. "Waffles with strawberries and whipped cream?"

"Absolutely! Would you like some bacon, eggs, hash browns...?" Krissy continued.

"Those all sound great," Mom replied, her stomach growling loudly.

I wondered when the last time was that she'd eaten. That any of the three of them had eaten. "Krissy, do you know when Dr. O'Leary's coming today? I want to ask him about Dad and Shep eating. They have all those stitches to worry about and have been sedated on and off...."

"I'll get you his number, Miss Kent," she responded before bounding off to get my mother breakfast.

I was nearly finished, so I stood up and took my plate to the kitchen. "I'm going to go sit with Dad!" I called over my shoulder.

Camille put her hands on her hips when I got there. "You did not clean your plate, young lady."

"Er...." I fidgeted awkwardly. "No. I didn't. I'm going to go sit with my dad."

She huffed and suddenly slapped together an egg-and-bacon sandwich on toast. "You'll eat at least half of that while you're sitting with him. Can't have all of you losing your strength."

I took the sandwich, not daring to argue with her. "Thank you. I'll finish at least half."

"Good. I'll have Krissy pop her head in to give you Dr. O'Leary's number."

"Thanks, Camille," I said.

She went back to mustering the troops as the day staff began to arrive, also forcing food on them.

I had to smile as I went to my parents' bedroom. It was pretty dark in there. The shades were cracked a little bit, but only just enough to see. "Dad?" I asked softly, seeing he was awake and staring in my direction.

"Hey sweetheart." He sounded groggy and a little out of it.

"Dr. O'Leary give you something to help with the pain?" I could see the angry, stitched red scar on his chest better now.

"Uh-huh. It's niiiice," my dad grinned.

Oh dear. "Really? That's nice. Did he say you should take it on an empty stomach?"

Dad shook his head. "No. But I wasn't hungry, so...."

I groaned. "Daaaaad."

He grinned. "I feel great."

"I'm sure you do."

Krissy poked her head in. "I've got Dr. O'Leary's number." She rattled it off.

I took out my phone and punched it in, saving it to my contacts before dialing. "Thank you, Krissy."

"You're welcome!" she trotted off again.

Dr. O'Leary sounded very tired when he answered. "Miss Kent?"

I paused. "How did you know it was me?"

"Tracy called ahead. She said she thought of reminding you that she has my number, but she didn't want to 'interrupt your flow.' I take it things are a bit rough over there?" he said.

Tracy. *Ugh, I am an idiot!* "Yeah. And my dad's been taking his pain meds without food," I explained. "He's... a bit loopy."

"I imagine he is." Dr. O'Leary sounded testy.

"Narc," Dad muttered.

"I'll come by in about two hours. In the meantime, see if you can't get your father and Mr. Pope to eat something light," the doctor said.

"I'll try," I responded. "Thank you, doctor. I know we've been... a lot."

"Not my usual, but sometimes it's good to be thrown a challenge every once in a while," he said with a small laugh.

I gave a little laugh, too. "We aim to please."

"I'll see you soon." He hung up.

I put my phone in my pocket. "Well, Dad, do you want some toast?"

He pouted. "Do I have to?"

"Oh, definitely. I'll go get you some toast with butter. Don't worry, I'm not just punishing you. Shep's getting some, too," I said, patting his shoulder before going back to the kitchen.

Tracy passed me with a plate of toast, heading for Shep's room.

"Um... sorry about blanking on Dr. O'Leary's number. I feel so stupid," I sighed.

She just grinned. "I just figured you needed to see it through on your own. We're all a bit jumbled today."

"Thanks for being here, Tracy. It means a lot. Even though you really should have gone home," I said.

"What can I say? My dad was never very interested in my brains, and finishing school doesn't have a course on 'Hell in a Handbasket 101.' If it turns out to be something stupid, well, I'll at least go out feeling as though I did the right thing," she replied proudly.

"I feel the same way," I admitted.

Tracy nodded and continued to Shep's room.

As I passed the dining room, I could see Mom still wolfing down food. I was glad, but also incensed. *What did they do to my family?* Clearly not fed them.

Camille wordlessly held out a plate of toast and some water when I got to the kitchen. "I hope this settles your father's stomach."

"You're psychic, Camille. Truly." I took the items.

When I looked back into the dining room, my mother was hunched over, asleep.

I smiled and began walking back to their room.

Then, I heard a loud thud behind me.

I set the toast and water down on an end table. "Mom? Did you fall over?" I walked back toward the dining room.

Mom was still in her chair.

Frowning, I kept going to the kitchen, only to find Camille on the floor with Krissy standing over her.

"Krissy! What happened?!" I gasped, going to Camille's side. "Oh my God!" Blood was pooling slowly under her head.

"She got in the way," Krissy said coldly, a complete turnaround from her earlier, bubbly self.

My blood froze. "In the way of what?"

"This." She pulled a gun from behind her back. "Don't worry, I didn't shoot her. I am going to shoot you."

"Why?" I asked, leaning back against the counter.

"You know why," she scoffed. "Your boyfriend pissed him off."

"You're going to have to be more specific. We've pissed off a lot of people," I said, quietly feeling behind me for something—anything—I could use against her.

Krissy snorted. "Why am I not surprised? Let's just say I'm going to tell Mr. Masterson that Mr. Freeborn sends his regards."

Ah. Ike.

White hot rage boiled up in me, scorching my nerves from head to toe. I was so tired of this shit!

I grabbed the frying pan on the stove next to me and heaved its contents at her.

Eggs slapped her right in the face.

Krissy shot and missed as she wiped eggs out of her eyes.

I didn't hesitate. I grabbed the pan's handle with both hands and swung at her like I was batting for the Yankees.

Her skull made a sickening crack and she pitched backward from the force of my blow, slamming the back of her head on the edge of the counter before crumpling to the floor.

Ignoring her prone form, I knelt down next to Camille and shook her shoulder gently. "Camille?"

Camille groaned and blinked slowly. When her gaze sharpened on me, she grabbed my wrist. "Miss Kent! You have to get out of here! Krissy... she's trying to kill you!" She began struggling to get up.

I pushed her back down. "Wait until the doctor comes. And... I don't think Krissy is going to be a problem anymore."

She turned her head slightly in the direction I was looking.

"I'm really sorry I made a mess in your kitchen..." I apologized.

Camille harrumphed. "She couldn't even crack an egg. Waste of space, that one."

I couldn't help myself. I burst out in hysterical laughter.

She touched my hand. "It's going to be all right, Miss Kent. I'll stay here on the floor and wait for the doctor, but you should check on your mother."

Mom was not asleep, then. "I'll make sure Dr. O'Leary comes quickly." I wiped tears from my eyes as I rose to my feet.

"I'll let you know if this one has the temerity to still be alive," she said.

"Thank you." I hurried out to the dining room, yanking my phone out of my pocket. "Dr. O'Leary? We've had a situation. I need you to come right now."

17

IKE'S REGARDS

"You're a jackass, Will Masterson," Bran said, speaking for the assembled gentlemen in my office.

I was surprised they let him speak at all. "Probably. But I'm not a baby-snatching, environment-raping, child-killing, drug-running sonofabitch."

"Oh, get over yourself," he snorted. "Everything a business does hurts somebody. Financially. Environmentally. Whatever. We might as well make money at it."

"Whatever helps you sleep at night," I quipped. I looked around at the others. "Is this an intervention or something?"

"Something like that," Cassian said. "We want to make sure you know you can't change things just because you want to. Whatever contracts you signed from your grandfather are ironclad. And I'm sure Ike told you what will happen if you start getting heroic."

"Ah." I nodded. "This is about Ike. I decided he was no longer necessary. We had a difference in vision for this company."

Don raised an eyebrow. "That's an understatement. Unfortunately for you, his was the right vision. There's nothing you can do about that."

"I don't care about his vision," I said flatly. "Or your threats. So, if that's all you're here for, all of you can go back to your respective offices and sit on it and spin."

Joel scowled at me. He wasn't the only one. "Will, I don't think you understand the gravity of your situation. Even if you do find some loophole to wriggle out of, you know that all of us, with all of our resources, are going to oppose you."

"Then, I guess I'd better make sure I drain as much of your resources as possible," I replied sweetly.

"I knew he wasn't going to take us seriously," Heath muttered.

"He will. He just doesn't know it yet," Morgan said.

I turned to him. "We're enjoying having your daughter stay with us. She's a wonderful guest. Maybe we'll make it permanent. She seems to be very Team Will."

Morgan ground his teeth. "Keep her. She's obviously disappointed in every one of my expectations. I have no desire to keep funding her lifestyle."

"Glad to hear it. Now, if you gentlemen will excuse me, I have a loophole to find," I said, making a shooing motion with my hand.

Bran grinned and it pulled at his pink scars. "At least Ike's not going after her."

I paused in my paging through documents. "Pardon?"

"Ike. You didn't think he'd just sit by and take it, did you?" Bran chuckled. "God, Will, you're so naïve."

"Bran, must you ruin every surprise?" John asked.

"What? I didn't say *what* he was getting," Bran grinned.

"What am I getting?" I responded, my voice as dark and threatening as I could make it.

"Ooh, he's mad. Maybe next time, he won't turn on his friends," Bran said.

"None of you are my friends." I would have said more, but my cell phone began to ring.

"That'll probably be the delivery person," Bran told me.

I snatched up my phone, checked the ID, and answered. "McKenzie?!"

The gathered men looked at each other with expressions varying from smug to discomfort.

"We've had an incident at home," McKenzie said, sounding tired. "Ike sent an assassin to kill me. She infiltrated the staff. She even knocked Mom and Camille out to get to me. Dr. O'Leary is here now. I... um... I killed her with a frying pan. It was kind of gruesome."

"I'm coming home right now," I replied. "Don't leave the house."

"Okay. I love you." She hung up.

As calmly as I could, I grabbed my suit jacket off the back of my chair and slipped my phone into a pocket. "If you'll excuse me, gentlemen, I have another engagement."

"She's alive?!" Bran balked.

"She is. Ike's friend isn't, but I'm not crying over that." I pushed through the men and headed for the door.

"How is she alive?!" Bran asked, flabbergasted.

I smiled slightly as I opened my office door. "She has quite a sting." Then, I left them there, walking as calmly through the office as I could.

When I got to the parking ramp, I ran to my BMW, ripping open the door and throwing myself inside. I tore out of the ramp and onto the street, cursing downtown traffic as I made my way out of Minneapolis. I took the highway out to Minnetonka, forcing myself not to speed too much. Getting pulled over would only slow me down.

Security at the Masterson Estate had the gate open before I turned the corner onto our lane. They were toting AK-47s and gave me a nod as I pulled in, closing the gates behind me.

I squealed into the turnaround by our front door and barely put the car in park before throwing the keys at Dan, our new chauffeur.

Once I ran in the house, the door of which being held open by none other than Camille, McKenzie slammed into me like a small brick wall.

I wrapped my arms around her, ducking my head so I could breathe in the scent of her hair. "Oh, love. I'm so glad you're safe."

"I don't know about 'safe,'" she mumbled into my shirt. "But we're all alive. Well, except Krissy, but she's kind of supposed to be dead."

"She's quite dead," Dr. O'Leary added, passing us with a covered gurney. "You won't have to worry about her anymore. She's going to be a Jane Doe, buried at the back of a hospital morgue."

"Thank you, Doctor," I said.

"Your lives are quite exciting, I have to say. I have a friend who is a private physician for the mafia, and he never gets this much action. It's nice to have bragging rights," he replied, trying to put me at ease.

I appreciated the effort. "Thanks."

"You're welcome." He continued pushing the gurney out.

Two household guards took the gurney from him, and Dr. O'Leary trotted back into the house.

I saw the back of Camille's head as she closed the door and the gauze there was thick and dotted with blood. "I'm so sorry, Camille," I said, still holding McKenzie tightly.

Camille shrugged. "The job does come with hazard pay. I was curious about that clause. But, hey, I have a car payment coming up."

"I'll buy you the damn car," I promised.

She smiled. "Even better. Don't worry yourself too much, sir. Everyone who matters is okay."

"Your mom?" I asked McKenzie.

"We laid her on the sofa and she woke up just a little bit ago. Whatever she was given wasn't that strong, according to Dr. O'Leary, but he sent a blood sample for examination, anyway," McKenzie said.

"Okay. That's good." I kissed her hair. "I wish I'd been home."

"You have work you need to do at the office, or this is going to keep happening," she pointed out.

I groaned. "But I don't want to leave you here."

McKenzie sighed. "You can't bring me with you. Someone has to stay here and watch over everyone else. Besides, this place is probably safer than your office."

"I sure thought so," I grumbled.

"Sir, it's lunchtime. Let's get you something to eat," Camille said quietly. "If you're going back to the office—"

"Not today. Tomorrow. But not today," I replied.

"You still need to eat," McKenzie urged me. She wriggled out of my arms and took me by the hand. "What's for lunch, Camille?"

"Tuna casserole," she said, leading us back toward the kitchen. "With mixed vegetables and rolls."

"Sounds delicious." I could see two new staff in the kitchen prepping plates.

Camille picked one up and handed it to me. "My mother's recipe. I hope you enjoy it."

"I'm sure I will."

McKenzie took another plate and we went to sit in the dining room. I was still a bit shaken, and it showed after they filled my glass and I went to take a sip, my hand trembling so hard I nearly spilled the wine.

"We're really okay," she said, reaching out and taking my other hand. This, of course, revealed a tremor of her own.

I had to laugh. "We're quite the pair."

"Well, Ike is an asshole. We probably should have seen this coming," she sighed.

"I did! That's why I turned over the whole staff!" I shook my head. "But he's a devious little fuck, I'll give him that."

"You don't think anyone else is a plant, do you?" She bit her lip.

"I... don't know. I don't know any of these people. I don't think so. I thought I vetted them well but... I guess I fucked up," I said.

"If you didn't catch them, I don't think anyone else could have," she responded loyally.

I kissed her temple. "Thanks, honeybee. But I still feel responsible."

"Then, buy Camille her car." She smiled at me. "And maybe, when this is all over, we take a honeymoon somewhere really nice, that we both want to see. As long as you still have money and it's not too expensive."

"When this is over, we're *moving* somewhere really nice that we both want to see," I assured her. "I'm retiring. If we have to move to the moon, we're getting away from all of this bullshit. Forever."

"Well, as long as we can bring my parents. And Tracy and Shep, if they want to go," she said.

"Of course." I squeezed her hand. "I don't suppose you'd mind going to college abroad? I know you had plans at the U of M...."

She laughed and kissed me. "I'll go to college on the moon if that's what it takes to stay with you."

I smiled and wrapped an arm around her.

Camille poked her head in the dining room and sighed. "I know you're feeling very lovey-dovey right now, but the casserole is getting cold."

We both jumped. "Sorry, Camille." I laughed sheepishly. "I do want to try it."

McKenzie quickly put a forkful into her mouth. She closed her eyes and made 'yummy yummy' noises.

I grinned and also tried a bite. It was amazing! "Camille, this is incredible!"

Camille beamed. "Excellent. I'm glad you like it. And you need to stop worrying about us here. As you can see, we can handle anything your enemies throw our way."

"It sure does seem that way," I admitted.

18

FRYING THE BIG FISH

McKenzie

Will stayed the rest of the day, which was nice but also counter-productive to our plans. I told him over and over that we had things handled on the home front.

It didn't stop him from poking his head in people's rooms under the pretext of checking in, but really it seemed he was looking for assassins to descend from the ceiling.

He brought me with him everywhere. All over the house.

On his third round of seeing my parents in three hours, I finally stopped him. "Will," I said, putting my hands on his chest. "Enough. There's nobody here but the people who are supposed to be here."

"I thought that before, too," he grunted, but held my wrists and leaned into my touch. "I love you. I don't want anything to happen to you."

"I feel the same way. I worry about you being in that building without anyone on your side. That I'll open my social media and it'll say 'businessman falls down elevator shaft in Masterson Building,'" I argued. "I dread that, and you've only been there one day! And not even a whole day!"

Will nodded. "Okay. I understand."

"So, take me with you. I know Tracy and Camille can keep things under control here. And besides, if I'm not here, none of the others are in danger. It seems like Ike just wants to punish you by killing me. It's just me we need to worry about," I reasoned. I rubbed my thumbs in little circles on his chest. "Please?"

He sighed and tapped his forehead to mine. "You're mean, you know that?"

"Did I get my way?" I asked.

"Yes. God help me," he muttered.

I smiled and kissed him. "Maybe I need to be mean more often."

"But you're going to either be by me or locked in my office. No wandering around," he said sternly.

"I won't. I promise." I kissed him again. "Maybe while you're in meetings and stuff, I can be looking through your computer. I can help."

"Hm." He looked thoughtful. "That's not actually a bad idea. I get pulled in so many different directions, it's been hard to find that information again."

"Leave it to me," I said confidently. "I'll find it!"

Will chuckled and pulled me into a hug. "I have no doubt."

"So, what would make you feel better?" I asked, hugging him back.

"Feel better?" he repeated.

"About today. So you stop looking for ninjas in the ceiling," I said.

He laughed again. "Okay, maybe I'm going a bit overboard."

"A bit."

His hand slid down to cup my ass. "But I can think of one thing that would make me feel better."

"Then, let's go." I pulled away just enough to take his hand and drag him down the hall to our suite.

As soon as the door shuts, his hands are all over me. He backs me up against the door and kisses my neck while shoving impatient hands up under my shirt and bra.

"Somebody's keen," I laugh, then groan, all thoughts of humor chased from my mind as he rolls my nipples between his fingers.

"I've been waiting over half the day to get my hands on you. Obviously, I'm 'keen.'" He strips my top and bra over my hand and tosses them aside, palming my breasts and bending to deliver a long lick across my nipples.

"You don't play fair," I gasped, my hand fisting in his hair.

"I'm about to get even less fair," he purred and hooked his thumbs in my waistband, pushing down my shorts and panties.

"Will!" I know where he's going and clamp my legs together. "If you make me come…."

"When I make you come," he corrected me.

"I'll fall on you!" I protested.

He grinned up at me as he kissed my belly. "What a way to go."

"Ugh, you silly goose!" I tugged on his hair, trying to redirect him.

Will wouldn't budge. "Open your legs for me."

"I don't think that's a good ide—"

He licked my belly. "Please?"

Will's pleading struck a chord in me, and I sighed. "Don't say I didn't warn you." I spread my legs.

"That's the stuff," he groaned and licked up my dripping wet seam.

I whimpered, my fingers still tangled in his hair.

"Talk to me, honeybee. Tell me how much you like it," he murmured against my mound.

"I-I like it." It was the understatement of the century, but it was what I could manage.

He poked his tongue inside me.

I moaned. "Will…."

When he gave it a swirl, my knees trembled.

"You can't," I said, teeth chattering. "It's too good…."

He was merciless. He began sucking on my clit, slipping his fingers into my passage.

I came hard, crying out his name, my knees buckling. I slid down the door.

Will was quick to get out of the way and caught me before I hit the ground. "I think it's time that I logged some time inside you," he murmured, lifting me up in his arms.

"You aren't expecting me to time you, are you?" I panted as he gently laid me down in the middle of the bed.

"Why bother? You know I'm having you more than once." He grinned at me.

I snorted. "You're probably having me more than four times. You are completely insatiable!"

"You like that about me." He pulled off the tie that had been hanging loosely around his neck and tossed it aside.

I had a feeling every stitch of clothing he was wearing was worth more than my first car, but he tossed his stiff white shirt aside, and his pants, and his boxers as though they were nothing.

"Shouldn't you, I don't know, fold those or something?" I asked absently. My attention was more focused on his massive cock, which was pointing right at me.

"Do you really want to wait for me to tidy up?" he countered.

I swallowed hard. "No, not really."

"I didn't think so." He got on the bed and prowled over my body.

I spread my legs, cradling his hips between my thighs.

Will reached to push his fingers inside me, but I stopped him with a hand on his arm. "I'm ready," I whispered.

He nodded and lined himself up, pressing his tip into my entrance. Then, he grasped my hand and kissed me while shoving himself inside me with one strong thrust.

I made a sound in my throat, half desire, half protest. Maybe I should have let him loosen me up a little more?

When he thrust a second time, though, I no longer cared. He was forcing my body to take him, and with every thrust afterward, my body happily obliged.

"There we go," he said after a few minutes. "I knew we'd get there."

"H-huh?" I asked, my breath coming in short puffs of need.

"Never mind." He kissed me again, long and slow, while thrusting a bit faster, though still powerfully and deep.

I ran my fingers through his hair, then wrapped my arms around his neck and clung to him for dear life as he picked up the pace.

Will reached between us and began thumbing my clit. "Come for me, honeybee. Let me hear you."

It was all too much. There was no way to stop it. And I didn't want to. "Holy-Will!" I screamed as one of the best orgasms I'd ever had tore through me.

He groaned as I tightened around his cock, then thrust deep and pumped me full of his cum.

When we were both finished, he collapsed on top of me.

I held him close, kissing his cheek, his forehead, his lips. Everywhere I could reach.

Will panted, but still fondled my breast.

"You can't possibly," I gasped, my sensitive nipple pearling under his touch.

"I figure by the time I get you riled back up, I'll be ready," he mumbled, moving his hips ever so slightly back and forth.

"You know that's not going to take much," I reminded him, as if he didn't already know.

"And you know I don't take much, either." He smirked at me.

"Brag much?" I smiled at him.

He nibbled my shoulder. "Just stating facts."

"Hm." I snuggled into him. "What if I decide to take a nap?"

"Then, I hope you like it while you're sleeping," he said. "Because I don't think I can stop."

I gave it some thought. "I don't mind."

"You don't mind?" he echoed.

"If you want to, I don't mind," I decided.

Will groaned. "Woman, you're going to be the death of me."

"But what a way to go," I quoted him from earlier.

He chuckled. "True." He went quiet.

"What are you thinking about?" I asked.

"All the times I got blue balls while you slept next to me when I could have just woken you up by giving you dick while you were sleeping," he sighed. "So many times."

I laughed. "Poor Will. Not getting laid nearly enough. Why, he only gets lucky three or five times a night! It's not fair."

"It's not." He fake pouted. Then, he nuzzled my neck. "It's never enough with you."

My cheeks heated up. "Now you're being a charmer."

"Is it working?"

I could feel his dick swelling inside me. "Well, something's working. I think someone's getting a little insistent."

"He just misses you." He continued kissing and nuzzling my neck while his hips began to move in earnest.

"He's right there inside me!" I laughed. "How can he miss me?"

"Mm." Will placed a hand next to my head and levered himself up on his arm so he had more freedom of movement as he thrust inside me. He stroked my cheek, then tucked a stray bit of hair behind my ear. "He always misses you, no matter where he is."

"Now you're just being silly," I scoffed.

"You're saying you don't miss him?" He winked at me.

I sighed and framed his face with my hands. "I just miss you. I miss you when you're gone. Terribly."

His soft smile melted my soul. "Me, too. I miss you, too." Then, he kissed me.

I kissed him back.

We made love. There was no other word for it. It was tender and perfect.

Tears slid down my cheeks as we came together, my body again accepting his release.

"I love you, McKenzie," he murmured in my ear.

"I love you, Will," I replied with a shuddering breath.

We quietly basked in each other for a long time.

Then, Will said, "You know I am going to have sex with you while you're sleeping, right?"

I giggled. "I kind of figured."

"Just wanted to make sure we were on the same page," he responded, kissing my hair.

"We're usually on the same page." I yawned. "Speaking of which, you might have an opportunity very soon."

He smiled. "Can't wait!" He started to move his hips again.

"Wait, I'm not even asleep yet!" I laughed.

"Like I said, can't wait," he countered.

I rolled my eyes. "Well, I suppose I could have *one* more mind-blowing orgasm. If I *must*."

"That's the spirit."

19

AT THE OFFICE

Will

McKenzie sat in my chair behind my wide desk, scrolling through folders and folders and drives of information. She hadn't found what she was looking for yet, but she was determined.

I sat at the conference table off to the side, staring down Grandfather's cronies. Again.

"We have an opportunity to rescue children from Gaza," Joel said.

"And by 'rescue,' you mean kidnap and put in the slave trade?" I inferred, feeling disgusted.

"It's better than them starving to death, Will," John pointed out.

"Barely." I honestly wanted to shower just from being in the same room as these men. It felt gross to have them here, gross to be on a first name basis after a month. Gross to be helping them rape the world.

"You really need to toughen up," Don said. "This is your life now. Deal with it."

Bran snickered. "He's always going to be a big marshmallow. You shouldn't even bother, Don."

"At least he gets things done." Cassian needled Bran.

Bran did not appreciate that. His scarred face turned red. "Listen, the Guatemala project—"

"Was an unmitigated disaster." Morgan scolded him.

"I've done other things!" Bran protested.

"Other disasters," Heath muttered.

"Hey, that weapons deal in Cambodia…" Bran began.

The other men just shook their heads.

"I think the general consensus is that you're an idiot, Bran," I said.

"Fuck you all," Bran snarled, standing.

"Where do you think you're going?" Morgan asked.

"Wherever the fuck I want, that's where! I don't need to sit here and be insulted!" Bran griped. He headed for the door.

"We should probably just eject him from the group," Cassian muttered as Bran walked out and slammed the door behind him.

"I'd be in favor," Joel said.

Morgan shook his head. "He knows too much."

"And if he ever disclosed it, this whole operation would fall squarely on his head. That's how it works." John shrugged. "I don't know if he's *that* much of an idiot."

"I wouldn't be surprised," I said.

There were nods of agreement all around.

"I suppose we could have him killed," Cassian mused.

"That's a little… extreme, isn't it?" I asked. "I mean, he's already scarred for life from that acid attack."

"Ike and your grandfather were masterful with that one. Too bad he didn't die like Gwendolyn," Morgan sighed.

Rage burned inside me. "Gwendolyn was a good person. She didn't deserve what happened to her."

I could hear the clicking had stopped back at my desk. I glanced at McKenzie and saw her face was pale. And angry.

"She was a busybody. She had no business poking around," Joel said.

"Or, as the kids say, she fucked around and found out," Morgan added.

Bile rose in my throat. I couldn't count the number of times these men had made me throw up. Not in front of them, of course, but often after meetings I had to go puke. They were just that sickening. "I suppose your next move is to throw acid on Tracy?"

McKenzie squeaked.

The men ignored her.

"There's no need to do anything that dramatic to Tracy," Morgan said. "She's just a victim of other people's bad decisions. She'll come around, eventually. Once she figures out what we do pays for her lifestyle."

"I think she'd rather live in a mud hut in the Congo than take your dirty money," I shot back.

Morgan scoffed. "She's more comfortable taking *your* dirty money, then?"

"I guess so. She's still living with me," I said.

Morgan's expression soured. "You are a real ass, Will Masterson."

"Thank you. I appreciate that, coming from you," I quipped.

"Gentlemen, can we get back to it?" John rapped his knuckles on an end table. "The sooner we get through business, the sooner we don't have to see each other again until next week."

I perked up. "You're giving me a week's reprieve?"

"We've finally managed to get through everything. Well, just about everything. Bringing you up to speed has been like crawling over broken glass," Cassian grumbled.

"I'm glad I've managed to make it difficult for you," I smirked.

"For the love of God, people, let's just wrap this up! I've got a meeting with a vendor I *cannot* reschedule for a fifth time!" Don yelled.

We all looked at him. "A vendor?" I asked.

Morgan snorted. "A tailor, more like. Did you out-girth another set of suits?"

Don's cheeks flushed, and I knew it was true. I had to bite the inside of my cheek to keep from snickering.

"I just want some new ones, that's all," he mumbled unconvincingly.

"Uh-huh." Morgan turned to John. "Why don't we just call it a day for now and come back tomorrow? I know we're all getting tired of this, but Will's being a dick, and I'm not sure any more is going to sink into that hard head today."

"Good point." John and the others glared at me.

"I can't tell you how sorry I am to be disrupting your lives," I said sweetly.

John rolled his eyes and stood. "Same time tomorrow?"

There were murmurs of assent all around.

"All right. Let's get out of here." John herded all of them out of my office. He looked back at me. "You need to get onboard, Will. Our patience will only last so long."

"And then what?" I challenged him.

"And then you might end up in worse shape than Hank Collins did when your grandfather had him crippled," John replied darkly.

Hank was crippled? He'd looked just fine to me up until the moment he'd been shot.

Maybe John didn't know that, whatever had happened, Hank had healed.

"Or maybe Bran," he mused.

I scowled at him. "Get the fuck out of my office."

"Gladly." He left.

McKenzie came around the desk and launched herself into my arms. This was the best part about her accompanying me to work. Comforting hugs.

The sick feeling in my stomach faded as I buried my face in her hair. As long as I could breathe in the sweet scent of her strawberry shampoo, and something that was just uniquely McKenzie, I could let everything else just fade away.

"You're a good man," she reminded me softly as we held each other.

"I don't feel like a good man," I mumbled.

She played with the ends of my hair, her fingertips brushing my neck. "I'm going to find it, Will. Everything we need. I promise."

"I know you are, honeybee. It's just a rough road between now and then." I pulled back a little and kissed her. "And it's not your fault at all if you can't. This company has so many files in so many places, and they probably moved them off the main server, anyway. They don't want us to find them."

"Tough for them. I'll go spelunking down in the file room, if I have to," she stated. "Or the archives. Or both. I'll pull every laptop, tower, company-issued cell phone, and tablet in this place. I will make people *cry*."

"Let's focus on making those assholes cry first," I said. "We're not even two-thirds of the way through all the files yet."

McKenzie drooped. "We're not."

"But we're going to get there. I mean, we're more than half and it's only been a month," I encouraged her.

"True." She still sounded bleak.

I tipped her chin up. "Hey. It's you and me against the world, right? We're going to be okay."

She hugged me again. "I want *you* to be okay."

"I am. I promise," I said, hugging her back.

McKenzie snorted. "Don't lie to me. We don't lie to each other."

I winced. "I will be okay?" I tried.

"Better. Now try to sound like you mean it," she said.

"I *will* be okay," I replied firmly.

She nodded. "I love you and I'm going to *make* it okay."

"That's my line," I argued.

"I'm stealing it. It's mine now. If you have to deal with those sleazebags, then I'm going to make this happen. You're already doing more than your fair share by entertaining them." She sounded very decisive.

"Well, it's no picnic, but that doesn't mean I shouldn't be helping in other ways. The more hands we have on deck, the faster this will go," I said.

McKenzie went quiet. "The more hands we have on deck."

"Yes... as in you and me," I responded.

She shook her head, then grinned up at me. "Tracy."

"What about Tracy?" I asked.

"Tracy can help!" she said excitedly.

"How?" I asked. "She's been holding down the fort at home."

"Camille can do that. No, she could go into her dad's office and look there, too!" she smiled.

I stared at her. "I'm not sure that's such a good idea...."

"It's a fantastic idea!" She gave me a spontaneous kiss. "She can just go groveling back home and get on one of her dad's devices and bingo! I'll bet none of it is hidden from him."

"That sounds... very dangerous, McKenzie. We can't protect her there," I said.

"Tracy's very good at protecting herself. Besides, we'll just ask. If she thinks she'll be in danger, we'll call the whole thing off." She patted my cheek. "It'll be okay, either way. I promise."

I wasn't sure I liked the idea of my sister being out there all on her own. Then again, I hadn't liked the idea of McKenzie being in the office and away from the Fort Knox that was our home, but it had actually turned out to be a godsend.

"I'm just worried she'll go in regardless of any danger. She's kind of reckless," I reminded her.

"Hm. True." She laid her cheek on my shoulder. "It was just a thought."

She sounded so defeated that I couldn't help but give in. "We'll ask her."

Her head came up. "But you just said—"

"I know. But, like you said, we have to try everything." I led her back over to my office chair. "I'm going to take my laptop and go work at the table on the day-to-day. You stay here and keep sifting through files on the shared drives."

"Okay." McKenzie started going through more folders. "Too bad we can't have office sex."

I paused, laptop under my arm. "Who says we can't?"

"Well, I mean, it probably wouldn't be appropriate for a CEO to bang his fiancée over his desk, especially during business hours," she laughed as though it was the silliest idea ever.

I didn't think it was so silly. I dropped my laptop back down on the desk hard enough that both the laptop and the desk made warning noises of protest.

"Will, you're going to crack the case!" she objected.

"I'd like to circle back to the desk sex idea. I have several points in its favor," I said, wheeling her chair back and pushing the keyboard aside so I could face her for a serious discussion. I also cued the door to lock and the glass to fog over.

"Oh?" She folded her arms over her chest. "And what might those be?"

I tugged off my tie. "One, it's a great way to relieve the tension we've been feeling and to purge the bullshit we've been dealing with today."

She nodded. "Go on."

"Two, we're both healthy, consenting, *engaged* adults and it would be a real shame not to christen my office," I said.

"Christen? None of your old girlfriends got to have sex with you here?" she replied, incredulous.

I shook my head slowly, holding her gaze as I unbuttoned my shirt. "You're the only person I've ever wanted to mix business and pleasure with."

"Lucky me." She unbuttoned her lavender blouse just enough that I could see the top of her lacy white bra. After a long pause, she asked, "Was there a third point?"

"Probably, but I can't remember. I'm in boob land now. And I know I'm really going to like the rides," I said, shrugging out of my shirt.

"They have some pretty wild rides there," she agreed with a straight face. "But can you afford the admission?" She slipped open her blouse to her waist, letting me see how her nipples had already hardened beneath the flirty, lacy fabric of her bra.

My cock strained in my pants. "What's the price of admission?" I wheezed.

McKenzie puckered her lips.

"You've got yourself a deal," I said and pulled her against me. I crushed my lips to hers.

20
TAKING DICK-TATION

McKenzie

Will turned me and braced my hands on the desktop. "Hold on tight," he murmured in my ear.

"I thought you wanted to go to boob land," I teased, anticipation igniting under my skin as he dragged the zipper down on the back of my pencil skirt.

"I want to visit all the parks today." He slipped his hands into the waistband of my skirt, hooking my panties with his fingers, and dragged both down my legs to rest on the floor. "I'm going to need you wider than that."

With a hard swallow, I said, "R-really?"

"Oh yes." His firm hand wrapped around my calf. "Step."

I lifted my leg and stepped where his hand put me. I started toeing off my heel.

"No, no, no. Shoes stay on. For now," he said, stopping me.

I turned my head to look at him. "Bossy, much?"

"We're in my office. I *am* the boss," he grinned back.

"All right, fine. What else do you want me to do, Mr. Masterson?" I asked.

He made a face. "Never call me that again, that's what. When I'm Mr. Kent, go crazy."

"Mr. Kent?" I repeated.

"I thought it had a nice ring to it." He rubbed his hand up under my shirt, along my spine.

My cheeks flushed at the idea of Will taking *my* name. But there was also something perfect about it. 'Kent' wasn't my parents' real name either, but it represented a life they wanted to build together. "I think I like Mr. Kent," I decided.

"Good." He grabbed my blouse at the collar.

I knew exactly what he wanted to do. "Oh no you don't! I'll take it off. *And* my bra. There is no way these are getting ripped to shreds!"

He leaned forward and I could feel him pout against my neck. "But Mr. Kent wants to."

"Mr. Kent has destroyed more of my clothes than I had in my closet to begin with!" I protested. "I like this blouse!"

Will pulled my blouse aside and kissed my shoulder. "Pretty please?"

His hand slid down between my legs to play with my clit.

"You're not even playing fair!" I moaned.

"I'll buy you three of them." He began negotiating with me.

"How many of them do you plan to destroy?" I countered.

"How often do you plan to wear them?" he asked.

"I really like that blouse." I squeaked as one finger delved inside me.

"Hm." He nuzzled my neck. "I suppose I might as well just get you an even ten, then. Have to support the garment industry."

I groaned, my fingers digging into the desktop. "Fine, you can do whatever you want, just please, *please* fuck me!"

"That's better." He tore my shirt apart.

I let the ends slide off my wrists, lifting one hand, then the other.

"Didn't I tell you to hold on?" he scolded me.

"Sorry, Mr. Kent. Would you like me to take dick-tation now?" I said in the most sultry tone I could muster.

"I would, but we still need to talk about the dress code in this office." He tugged on my bra, undoing the three hooks at the back until it fell open and dangled off my arms, setting my breasts free.

"Have I violated the dress code, Mr. Kent?" I asked.

"Yes." He opened a drawer near me and took out a letter opener.

I looked at it in confusion, my body tensing around his finger. "Will?"

"You're wearing too many clothes." Then he swiftly cut the straps on my bra so that fell on the floor, too.

"Will!" I gaped. "That was completely unnecessary!"

"Mr. Kent thought it was." I heard his zipper.

"Mr. Kent needs to learn some impulse control!" I huffed.

He set the letter opener back in the drawer and started finger-fucking me in earnest.

I leaned into my palms as my arms began to shake. "W-we are having a s-serious conversation when…."

"After you come. Right now, you need to take dick-tation." His fingers left, and I felt the big, wide head of him at my entrance.

"Sounds like a plan," I gave in.

Will pushed my legs apart a couple of inches with his knee. I was in desperate need and wanted to ride that leg, but I knew I was getting something better.

Once he had me where he wanted me, he began to push inside.

I whimpered, feeling him stretch me. It was always a bit of a struggle to take him, and that never seemed to end no matter how often we had sex. The man just filled me all the way up. There was nothing either of us could do about it.

"Deep breaths," he managed to tell me, his dick sinking in deeper and deeper.

My fingers flexed against the desktop. I widened my legs another inch.

Then, he was in.

He blew out a long breath. "Is it okay, honeybee? Do you feel good?"

I nodded, feeling full to capacity. "It feels good… Mr. Kent."

Will chuckled, his hands palming my breasts as he kissed my shoulder. "So, you like taking dick-tation?"

"It's my favorite," I smiled back at him.

"Good. Because you're going to be taking lots of it. I have a really long memo I need to dick-tate." He pulled his hips back slowly.

I felt him slide almost all the way out of my body and made a small sound of protest.

"What an impatient secretary I have here," he purred, playing with my nipples.

"It's called an executive assistant—!" I ended on a squeal as he slammed into me, filling me up once more.

"Hush, Mrs. Kent. You're taking dick-tation. I only want to hear you moan," he said hotly in my ear.

"You're a mean boss." But my heart melted when he called me 'Mrs. Kent.'

"You have no idea. I might even work you overtime." He thrust again. Then again.

It was too slow. I wanted—no, *needed*—more. "Mr. Kent? Please can you dick-tate a little faster?"

He gave my shoulder a soft bite. "So needy, Mrs. Kent. Do you have other things to do?"

"I was thinking of organizing my desk," I replied flippantly, hoping that might have some effect.

It did. Suddenly, he was thrusting so hard and fast that I could hear and feel his balls slap against me.

"The only desk you need to worry about is the one you're bent over right now," he growled, giving my nipples a painful pinch.

It sent a zing all the way through my body, but especially to my core. "M-my mistake, Mr. Kent," I gasped.

My palms squeaked against the desktop from the force of his thrusts, and I had to fight to keep them in place.

"You bet your ass that was a mistake. Next you're going to tell me we shouldn't fuck on that sofa over there. Or against the window behind us. Hell, there's a perfectly serviceable conference table on that side of the room. I'd love to see you all messy and spread open for me on it," he grunted, drilling me like a machine.

I had to needle him, if I could find the breath for it. "So… no organizing my desk, then?"

Will reached down and thumbed my clit. "I'm going to burn that fucking desk."

I laughed, then moaned as he rode me hard right into a shattering orgasm.

He groaned as I clenched around his cock and exploded inside me.

As we stayed there, panting, I couldn't stop a little imp that rose up in me. "I suppose I can go organize my desk now," I said with a dramatic sigh. "Taking dick-tation is quite a job."

"I'm not finished with you yet," he rumbled. He pulled out, then scooped me up in his arms.

I wound my arms around his neck. "Really? There's more dick-tation?"

"I thought of another memo," he said as he walked across the room and laid me on the conference table.

We had sex there, with the cool glass chilling my back, then against the office windows, which caused a different kind of chill. We ended up on one of the leather loveseats before Will finally needed a rest. I did, too.

"What time is it?" I asked, looking out the window. My phone was back on his desk.

Will tiredly checked his watch. "Late afternoon. About three-twenty."

I sat up, nearly knocking heads with him. "We did it all day?!"

"We sure did," he grinned, sitting up as well.

"But… the files…" I mumbled.

He kissed me. "One afternoon in a month's time isn't going to make a difference."

I drooped. "True. I haven't found anything in a month."

"You will," he assured me, and hugged me to him. "We both need a break every once in a while, though, or we're going to burn out and miss things."

"I suppose that's true." I hated to think of myself glossing right over the files I was looking for just because I was too exhausted to see what was right in front of my eyes.

Will rubbed the nape of my neck. "I love you. And we've both been looking for those files and not found them. That's not something you can take sole responsibility for."

"You're also entertaining those assholes," I pointed out. "You're doing a lot more than I am."

He snorted. "I wouldn't say that. Every time I look up you're hunched over that keyboard, glaring a hole in the computer screen. Having those assholes show up just means I get a break. You don't."

"But they're so… slimy." I made a face. "I feel like I need a shower just from touching the same doorknob they did."

"Maybe we should have sterilized the table before I fucked you on it," he mused. "You're right; they are slimy."

I touched his cheek. "You didn't throw up today."

Will kissed my hand. "I had you. And I *had* you." He grinned mischievously.

I swatted him. "Glad I could help."

"You know what would help more?" he asked, his eyes twinkling.

"What?" I asked.

He inclined his head toward the en suite bathroom. "Shower sex."

"Oh my God, I can't believe you have anything left!" I gaped.

"Like you said, I'm incorrigible." He stood and reached for my hand.

I looked down and saw he was already rock hard. "I suppose it would be mean not to take care of that for you." I sighed. "An executive assistant's job is never done."

"Secretary," he corrected me, his lips twitching.

"I know you don't call Roseline that," I said of his new assistant. "At least I hope you don't."

"Of course not! She's my executive assistant, not my secretary!" he replied.

"What's the difference?" I asked, taking his hand.

Will pulled me flush against his body so his straining cock folded up between us. "Secretaries take dick-tation."

I swatted him again. "Chauvinist."

He captured my hand and kissed my fingers one by one. "A man's entitled to his fantasies."

"Oh really? And what all do you fantasize about?" I raised an eyebrow.

"You." Then, he kissed me.

21

FAVORS FROM FRIENDS

"Basically, we need you to go back to your father's place and pretend as though you're sorry and want to be a good daughter," I said slowly, sitting in front of my sister with McKenzie at my side. "While you're there, you might be able to find the files we're looking for. I'm sure they have to be shared somehow among all of those—"

"Sleazeballs," Tracy provided, making a face. "Ugh. Yes, I'll do it."

I blinked. "We haven't talked about the danger yet."

She waved a hand. "He's my father. I'm hardly in any danger. I might be under house arrest for a while, but that's just going to make it easier to go snooping."

McKenzie gave me a pained look. "Um… Tracy… it is very dangerous. You can say no. Or at least, you know, discuss the…."

"I've got it handled, don't worry. So, do I go in with a burner phone?" Tracy sounded excited.

"I knew this was a bad idea," I muttered to McKenzie.

"Too late now," McKenzie whispered back.

"I suppose a burner phone would be a good idea," I said more loudly. "But I really think you should give this more consideration."

Tracy was quiet for all of thirty seconds, her head tilted to the side. "Done! Okay, burner phone...."

Shep walked into the room, still a bit careful of his abdomen, but otherwise in good shape. "What are we talkin' about?"

"Burner phones," the three of us said together.

"Why do we need burner phones?" he asked, his eyes narrowing.

"I'm going to go spy on my dad!" Tracy replied excitedly.

"Fuck." Shep lowered himself into a chair next to us. "Are you fuckin' out of your mind?!"

Tracy shrugged. "We need files. They haven't been able to find them. It's been a month. Now, we're on to Plan B."

"Plan B? *Plan B?!* Kid, do you have any idea how dangerous this is goin' to be for you?!" he shouted.

We all shrank back from his anger. It was surprising, coming from Shep.

Tracy squared her shoulders. "I'm not a kid."

"You are." Shep rubbed his face. "You're all kids and you shouldn't be dealin' with this shit."

"I am twenty-three years old," Tracy continued. "And I'm doing this. No, we shouldn't have to deal with it, but them's the breaks."

"I don't care if you're two-hundred-and-three... never mind. I already know what a stubborn mule you are." He turned to me. "I actually wanted to talk to you."

"Me?" I asked.

He nodded. "These two don't need to be here."

I frowned. "All right. McKenzie, how about you and Tracy start figuring out the details. Have one of the guards get us all some burner phones. I wouldn't be surprised if there's some sort of spyware on our personal phones by now."

"Okay." McKenzie gave me a hug. "We'll figure it out. See you later. You too, Shep."

"See you." He waited until the women had gone. "Will, I need to leave."

I stared at him. "What?"

"I need to get out of here. I'm sorry, I can't be along for the ride anymore." He sounded very serious.

He also didn't sound at all like himself, which wasn't strange given he'd lost his mother. But there was something… more… there.

"What are you planning to do, Shep?" I asked, my eyes narrowing.

With a slight smile, he shook his head. "Can't tell you. Looks like the world's made you paranoid. That's a good thing."

"It's not paranoia if it's real," I said. "Seriously, what are you going to do when you leave here?"

Shep stood. "Just wanted to let you know. I'm takin' one of your cars. Don't report it stolen."

"I won't. Can you wait until we get the burner phones, at least? I want to be able to check in and make sure you're okay," I replied.

"I ain't the one you need to worry about." His smile turned sinister.

I had no idea who had harmed him or his mother in another life, but I was scared enough on their behalf to want to pray for them. Almost.

"Tracy better watch her back. Fathers ain't always what they seem," he continued. "I'm gonna go get my bag, then I'm outta here."

My throat went dry. "You're going after Xavier Pope."

"I abso-fucking-lutely am," he seethed, clenching his fists.

In the grand scheme of things, I could see where his anger was coming from. But…. "He's still your father."

"Not anymore. Not any more than your granddad was your granddad." He headed for his room.

"Wait! Let me give you some money, at least," I said, scrambling to my feet.

Shep chuckled. "Already took some. Thanks."

"And a phone. Please wait for a phone. What if you need something?" I pleaded.

"Then, I'll take care of it myself. You're a good kid, Will. But you don't need to take care of me anymore. Check the news from time to time. You'll know where I've been," he said.

There was no arguing with him. I sagged. "All right. But at least call me from a pay phone if you need me."

"That I can do." He went down the hall and back to his room.

A minute later, he showed up with a large duffel bag slung over his shoulder. "Hopefully, I'm about to make your life a little easier."

"That would be appreciated, but not expected," I responded.

"Tell everybody I'll miss them," he said, swallowing.

"I will." I held out my hand for him to shake.

Shep grabbed my hand and pulled me into a bear hug, slapping me on the back. "I think we're past handshakes now."

"You're right," I agreed, hugging him back.

He let me go after a while and hefted his pack further up his shoulder. "It's been a wild ride."

"It has. Good luck, Shep." I gave him an encouraging smile.

"Good luck, Will." He took big strides through the house and out the front door.

I was certain the new chauffeur would point him in the right direction. There wasn't a car in the garage I wouldn't part with for Shep.

"Okay, you can stop eavesdropping now," I called.

McKenzie and Tracy, both teary-eyed, came out of the kitchen with Camille.

"They were helping me make a roast," Camille lied, her eyes also misty.

"Uh-huh." I opened my arms, expecting McKenzie, then suddenly I was holding three crying women.

"I liked Shep," Camille sniffled. "He was a real gentleman."

"He was. A diamond in the rough," Tracy agreed. "And I'm not crying. This is allergies."

McKenzie gave a wet laugh. "I have allergies, too."

"Fall must be coming," I agreed, feeling a deep sadness in my chest.

We all finally pulled it together.

"Well, that roast won't make itself," Camille said, whisking herself off to the kitchen.

"You weren't helping with the roast, were you?" I asked Tracy and McKenzie.

"Pfft. You wouldn't want to eat it if I had," Tracy scoffed.

"You really think Camille would let us touch anything in her kitchen?" McKenzie laughed.

I chuckled. "Good point. I'm going to keep my phone on at all times. If Shep gets into trouble, I want to be able to help."

"Stubborn asshat," Tracy grumbled. "Couldn't even wait for a burner phone. But I wish him well, just the same. I think each of us has our own axe to grind."

"We do." I gestured for the women to sit down again. I took my spot next to McKenzie and draped my arm around her shoulders. "Do you want to text your father and start laying the groundwork for being welcomed back into the fold?" I asked Tracy.

Tracy nodded and drew her cell phone out of her pocket. "Dear Criminal…" she smirked.

"Ha-ha. Make it believable," I said.

"I know. I was just messing with you." Tracy rolled her eyes and moved her thumbs rapidly over the letters.

McKenzie and I leaned forward, trying to see what she was typing.

Tracy grinned and pulled her phone back. "Give me a minute."

We sat back, both of us listening to the electronic click-click-click of Tracy's typing.

"Well?" I asked when I heard the swoop of the message being sent. My stomach dropped. "Shouldn't you have let us vet it first?"

"No need. But I can read it to you. 'Dad, this place is so awful. People just keep dying or disappearing around me and I can't even leave to take my mind off it. I just want to go shopping or to lunch or anything, ANYTHING that will get me out of this place! I… hate to say it, but I want to go home. Please.' Does that sound good?" Tracy replied.

I nodded. "That actually sounds fantastic."

"Don't sound so surprised. I've been a pampered princess for twenty-three years. If they taught me anything in finishing school, it was how to whine to Daddy for money," she said.

"Sounds like a first class education to me." I smiled, but I could tell Tracy didn't think it was funny.

"I didn't like being raised to be a vapid bimbo whose only use was finding a husband. Now, I've actually got a chance to make a difference." Tracy folded her arms over her chest. "I'm taking it."

"You're not a vapid bimbo," McKenzie said quickly. "Not even a little bit." She reached out and squeezed Tracy's hand.

Tracy sighed. "Sorry. I've got my own baggage. It doesn't always stay in the overhead compartments."

"I understand." I put my hand over McKenzie's so we were holding Tracy's hand together. "You're truly a marvel. Don't let anyone tell you that you aren't."

Tracy swallowed and wiped her eyes with her free hand. "Stupid allergies."

Garrett, who'd been working the guard station, came in then, holding three nondescript cell phones. "Burner phones, as you requested, Mr. Masterson."

"Thank you, Garrett, you can put them on the table. I'm surprised you were able to get them so quickly," I said.

He shrugged. "You just gotta know the right people."

"I'm glad you know the right people." I grinned.

"Me too. Give 'em hell, sir." Garrett walked back outside.

The three of us broke apart and each grabbed a cell phone off the table.

"Okay. Code names. We don't want anyone peeking over our shoulders to see who we're texting," Tracy said.

"Code, period. We can't openly discuss what we're doing," I responded.

McKenzie looked thoughtful. "Maybe we should talk about shopping. Like, save our names as stores and then talk about sales, BOGOs, discounts, things like that. It's something your father would expect to find on your phone, right?"

"Right." Tracy typed in a contact that said Louis Vuitton and another that said Cartier, taking down our numbers as we gave them to her.

"Who do you want to be?" I asked.

She grinned. "Gucci."

"Gucci it is." We saved her as a contact.

"So, Louis, what do we do n—?" Tracy began. Her phone made a fairy dust sound.

We looked down and, sure enough, Morgan Pope had responded.

Dad: *I'm sending a car. You'd better be in it. You're in big trouble, young lady. But I knew you'd see reason, eventually.*

"I'm definitely going to be under house arrest," Tracy groaned. "But, like I said, it just gives me more opportunities for snooping."

"We'd better get you packed up," McKenzie said. She stood, not looking happy about the situation.

I wasn't, either, but I was resigned to it. "Do you want me to help?"

"Um, no offense, Will, but I'd rather die than have my brother handling my underwear." Tracy gave a nervous laugh.

"Oh. Right." I watched her and McKenzie go down the hall to her room.

I sat back down on the sofa, holding my head in my hands.

This had to be the worst idea ever.

22

THE HUNT

McKenzie

Gucci: *Barbados bag marked down to $1,500 at all outlet stores.*

It was the same thing Tracy had been texting for two months. She hadn't found anything. And neither had we.

I was tempted to bang my head on Will's keyboard. I confirmed our lack of progress.

Cartier: *All watches 25% off at participating outlet stores.*

Will was out at the office at a meeting with legitimate businessmen, keeping the virtuous side of the business afloat. Still, he managed to text.

Louis Vuitton: *BOGO on specific purses at participating outlet stores.*

I could almost hear Tracy snickering. He probably had no clue that Louis Vuitton would be very unlikely to do a BOGO on its purses. But he'd at least put in the right words, "BOGO" expressing disappointment, and "outlet stores" stating he hadn't found anything, either. I wondered how he was even looking during a business trip. He was probably scouring his tablet after hours.

A knock sounded on the office door.

"Come in!" I called.

Roseline opened the door, looking rather flustered. "I'm sorry,

Miss Kent, but I couldn't stop him, and security won't come remove him—"

Bran clapped her on the shoulder and pushed her away. "That'll do, Roseline. I just need a few moments alone with Miss Kent. I won't be long."

It was at that moment I realized we should have discussed bodyguards with Will gone. "Bran, you're not welcome here," I said as he closed the door behind him.

"Please. You don't have to look so scared. I'm an engaged man," he grinned.

So, he'd come to gloat. "To Tracy."

"To Tracy. That was always the plan. You were just going to be a bit of fun. Not that you still can't be," he said.

Disgust made bile rise in my throat. "That's okay. I'd rather French kiss a frog."

"You're missing out." But he just shrugged, which made me slightly less wary.

"What do you want, Bran?" I asked.

"I'm just supposed to warn you. You've been digging for quite some time now. You need to stop," he said flatly.

"Oh, you've noticed, have you? We must be close, then." Outwardly, I was flippant. Inside, I started freaking out.

He was unimpressed. "You might be. You might not be. The answer is the same. Knock it off."

"No." I met his gaze, not backing down. "You can leave now."

"Oh, can I?" He walked forward instead, right up to the desk.

When he started coming around the side, I pushed back the chair and stood.

Bran grabbed my arm. "Not so fast, McKenzie. You know what I'm capable of."

"Pretty sure if you actually put hands on me, security *will* get off its ass and throw you out," I shot back, trying to wriggle out of his grip.

"Probably. But you could be dead by then. The only reason you're still alive is to keep Will under control." He squeezed harder. "But, since he knows about Tracy…."

Fear spiked through me. "Do what you want," I said with as much bravery as I could muster. "Will won't stop looking."

"Another reason it's useless to kill you," he sighed. "More's the pity. You are a huge pain in the ass." He yanked me closer and ran a finger down my cheek. "But a pretty one."

I bit his finger.

"Ouch!" He dragged his hand back. "My, you are a little bitch."

"Maybe you forgot how much of a bitch I can be. Shall I remind you?" I grabbed the letter opener off the desktop and slashed his scarred cheek.

He jumped back. "Fuck!"

I pressed the intercom. "Roseline, call security. I'm being attacked!"

"At once, Miss Kent!" she replied.

Bran growled and lowered his hand, which was bloody now. Blood dripped down his cheek, also smeared everywhere by his hand. "I think I will kill you."

I held the letter opener out in front of me. "I'd like to see you try."

He started to come at me, but the door banged open. Two security guards came in with their guns drawn.

"That's enough, Mr. Lockwood," one of them said.

Bran scowled at them. "She attacked me!"

"Sir, you're standing behind her desk. I find that very hard to believe." The security guards' guns didn't waver.

"But… she… I can explain…" Bran stuttered.

"Mr. Lockwood, you're going to need to come with us. We will escort you from the premises." The guards gestured for him to follow them.

Bran gave me a death stare. "This isn't over."

"I don't expect it ever will be," I responded.

He smirked. "That's the right attitude."

Honestly, even as they escorted Bran out, I felt defeated. I couldn't believe I'd admitted it out loud, but I was starting to feel like it was never going to end.

I took a deep breath and went back to the computer. There was only one way it *would* end, and that was if we could find the files.

Several hours later and no closer than I was before, I leaned my head on the desktop and started to cry.

There was another knock on the door.

I sat up and quickly wiped my eyes. "Roseline. Sorry, I was just having a rest."

She walked in and closed the door behind her. "You're not finding it either, are you?"

My heart was not going to survive this day. "What?"

"The files." She plopped down into a chair with a frustrated huff. "I've been looking since Mr. Masterson hired me and I still can't find them. I have noticed you, Mr. Masterson, and Miss Franz looking as well. No luck?"

"Who-who are you?" I asked.

"Let's just say one of the alphabet agencies," she replied evasively. "I'm beginning to doubt they're even there, honestly."

I shook my head vigorously. "No. Will's seen them."

"Maybe on a thumb drive?" she speculated.

"Roseline, telling me you're from the government without showing me a badge or anything doesn't make me feel any better. Why would I share information with you?" I asked. "And even if I did believe you, we haven't had a lot of luck with alphabet agencies on our end, so it wouldn't exactly be a point in your favor."

She nodded. "Fair enough."

I eyed her warily. "But... you do have a point about a thumb drive or some other external drive. We should start looking for that, too."

"I'd like permission to search your house," she said.

I blinked at her. "You did hear what I just said, right?"

"Camille knows what to look for, but even *she* hasn't found it yet," she sighed. "I think we'll need a whole team."

She might as well have stabbed me through the heart. "Camille?" I said faintly.

"Don't worry. She loves you to bits and pieces. For real. I'm always afraid she's been compromised, but you're good people, so I'm not terribly worried about it." She gave me a hard look. "You need out of this situation. We need to nail these bastards to the wall. Win-win."

"It's a joint task force, isn't it?" I asked tiredly.

"Good call. I'm FBI, but we're also working with ATF and DEA. And the DHS, of course. The CIA is waiting in the wings. These guys are going to be facing charges internationally. Interpol is going to have a field day with them," she said.

"You know your alphabet. Still doesn't mean anything to me," I replied, thinking of going home right then and confronting Camille.

"Smart. I like it." She took out her phone and put it on speaker. "Do you have him?"

"Yes, ma'am. Got him between meetings at the hotel," a man responded.

I had a bad feeling. "What have you done to Will?"

"Nothing. Just introduced ourselves. I couldn't exactly have a task force march in here to prove our identities to you," she said.

She had a point. Still…. "I want to talk to him."

"That was the idea. Put him on," she ordered.

"McKenzie?" Will's familiar voice echoed up out of her phone.

"Will! Are you okay? Did they hurt you?!" I asked, coming around the desk to get closer to the phone.

"They're fucking annoying, but no, they haven't hurt me." He sighed. "Just let them search the damn house."

I paused. "What?"

"We haven't gotten anywhere. Tracy's going to be forcibly married to Bran any day now. And we're surrounded by them anyway. We need something to happen. They might as well search the house," he said.

I frowned at the phone, then at Roseline. "I'll only let them search the house if you come home."

"Can do," she responded. "Any other demands?"

"That's the only one. I want to see him for myself." I looked down at the phone again. "Is it okay for you to come home now?"

"I'd basically wrapped up business here, so yes," he said. "I'll see you soon, love."

"Love you, too!"

Roseline disconnected the call.

Will sounded okay. Still, I wasn't going to relax until I saw him with my own eyes. "I guess we wait."

"I guess we do," she replied.

ROSELINE AND I DIDN'T SPEAK THE WHOLE THREE HOURS IT TOOK WILL to return. He walked into the office with two men in suits, chatting to them about mergers and stock prices.

Once the door closed, he stopped the act and walked straight to me.

"Are we screwed again?" I whispered in his ear as he hugged me.

"No. Just inconvenienced," he muttered. "All right, ladies and gentlemen, let's get this over with. We'll go to the house now."

"Excellent," Roseline said, rising from her chair. She smoothed down her skirt. "I can't thank you enough for your cooperation."

"Uh-huh." Will took my hand, and we walked out with the three of them, heading straight down to... another black SUV.

"Seriously?!" I hissed.

Will bit his lip, trying not to laugh. "The only way to travel, I guess."

"Ugh." I stomped over to the Tahoe and stomped inside, sliding across the seat so Will could get in as well.

He ended up in the middle seat because one of the alphabet agents got in the back next to him.

The other male agent got in the driver's seat while Roseline took the passenger seat.

"All cozy?" she asked.

"Like a sardine," Will replied, putting an arm around me after we'd put on our seat belts.

"You were quick to put those on," she said.

He gave her a bitter smile. "We have some experience with car accidents."

"Ah. True." Roseline took out her phone and started making calls, coordinating the search.

By the time we got to the estate, there was a whole slew of black vehicles outside the gate. Garrett and Eric and a few others were staring them down, holding AK-47s.

I appreciated their loyalty, but I didn't want them to get hurt. As soon as the SUV stopped, I jumped out and ran to the gate. "Stand down! Stand down!"

Garrett didn't move a muscle, even while the others reluctantly put down their guns. "Miss Kent, have you been kidnapped?" he asked in a very serious tone.

"No. These are government agents. They need to find something Mr. Masterson Sr. might have been hiding. I promise. I promise everything is okay," I said.

He waited another beat, then lowered his weapon. "All right, Miss Kent. But I'm gonna be on them like white on rice."

"I wouldn't expect anything less." Will walked up beside me and put a reassuring hand at my back. "I really wish you wouldn't jump into the middle of potential gun battles like that," he whispered in my ear.

"I didn't want anyone to get hurt," I replied.

"I don't want *you* to get hurt." He kissed my hair. "All right. Everyone, go inside. Please be aware that my security detail will be monitoring your movements."

"We'd really rather—" Roseline began.

He speared her with a harsh look. "That part's non-negotiable."

She blew out a long breath. "Okay, everyone. Go in and spread out. We're going to systematically search that place. No stone unturned, understand?"

"Yes, ma'am!" was the loud response.

23

NO STONE UNTURNED

Will

Garrett was the most dogged of my guards, popping his head into every room the joint task force was searching. Which was every room. There were even three people in the ceiling.

Dan was standing sentinel over the cars as five men scoured the garage and every vehicle in it.

Camille, though a member of the task force itself, still barked at those going through her kitchen, making them put things back exactly how she had them.

"Can we take the computers?" Roseline asked, sticking her head out of my grandfather's den.

"His computers? Knock yourself out," I called back, glad that she'd bothered to ask. I was pretty sure she didn't have to. "I managed to lock us out of those. Couldn't figure out the password."

"We'll work on that," she said as two men carried out Grandfather's tower, laptop, tablet, and phone.

They were also pulling books off the shelves and going through them.

"We might need to examine these further. Can we take them, too?" She looked up at me.

"Go ahead. If you can find anything we haven't, you deserve to have it," I said.

"Bartlett, get the books."

The man I assumed was Bartlett began coordinating with three other men to box up the books and carry them up.

Another man with gloves began feeling around the shelves.

I'd done the same thing weeks ago and found nothing. Still, I held my breath, hoping this man might have more luck.

He finished and shook his head.

Roseline touched her ear. I realized she had an earbud in. "We're just about done here," she said. "Kind of disappointing, but we'll see if we can get into his electronics."

"Sounds good," I replied with a disappointed sigh.

She squeezed my shoulder as she passed me. "We're going to get these guys. It's just a question of when."

My burner phone dinged.

"Sorry, that's Tracy checking in," I said, pulling my phone out and glancing at the screen.

"What does it say?" she asked.

Gucci: *I'm at Bran's. I found it! I'm locked in the bathroom with his laptop. He's coming. I'm scared. Help!*

My breath caught. "It says you need to go to Bran Lockwood's estate. Right now!"

Roseline glanced over my shoulder. Then she began barking orders. "Everyone wrap it up. We're going on a rescue!"

"I'm coming with you," I said. "Non-negotiable, or I'm going to get very difficult to deal with."

"No time to argue. Get in the Tahoe," she replied tersely.

I hurried through the house, grabbing McKenzie by the arm. "Tracy's in trouble. Take care of your parents. I'll be right back."

She winced and then I noticed the finger bruises on her arm. "Honeybee?"

"Bran came by the office. He did this. But don't worry, I got him back good," she said.

I sighed and kissed her forehead. "I don't have time to talk about it now. But we will later, okay?"

"Okay. Be safe." She gave me a quick hug, then went to her parents' room.

My blood boiled as I headed for the Tahoe. I jumped in just as they were about to take off. "Sorry. I had to figure something out about Bran."

"What's that?" Roseline asked, coordinating the rescue between talking to me.

"He's a dead man," I said flatly.

The guards at Bran's gate were not quite as loyal, and as soon as they saw badges and alphabet jackets and vests, they rolled out the red carpet.

Roseline insisted I wear a Kevlar vest. It was stiff, but I didn't care. I would have worn a clown nose and a tutu if it meant I could get to Bran. I was fed up to my hairline with his antics.

The task force rammed in the front door and ran right past the bewildered staff.

"Which bathroom?" Roseline asked.

"I don't know," I replied in frustration. I texted Tracy.

Louis Vuitton: *Which bathroom?*

Gucci: *Why don't you come and find me, Will?* :)

"Sonofabitch. He's got her." I showed Roseline my screen.

Her lips thinned. "Fan out. Find them. We've got a hostage situation."

"Yes, ma'am!" The task force spread out, walking cautiously with guns raised throughout Bran's mansion.

I went with Roseline and her two men. "If he's taunting me, I can only think of four places he would be. Kitchen, pool house, the bedroom he put us in when he drugged me, or the guesthouse."

She nodded slowly. "My money would be on the guesthouse. More places to hide."

"Sounds about right for that slippery little fucker," I agreed.

Still, we passed the kitchen on the way out the back door and checked it just in case.

Then, we crunched over the gravel, past the pool, to the guesthouse.

"Bran!" I called as one of Roseline's men kicked in the door. "Stop screwing around! It's over."

"Tell that to little miss snoops-a-lot. Where the fuck is it, Tracy?!" I heard a slap.

"Fuck you!" Tracy replied.

"Sonofabitch," I seethed. "Bran, I swear I am going to kill you myself!"

"Not a lot of incentive to stop playing hide-and-seek. But here, let's play a new game." He came out of an upstairs hallway holding Tracy in front of him. He pressed her against the railing, threatening to push her over.

"Sir, I'm going to have to ask that you step away from Miss Franz," Roseline said evenly.

Bran laughed coldly. "I'd really rather not. In fact...." He started pushing Tracy over the edge.

She gripped the railing, screaming.

I saw the fresh bandage on Bran's cheek and remembered what McKenzie said about 'getting him back good.' Now, it was my turn. "Bran, I swear to *God* if you hurt my sister, I will make you regret the day your father ever laid eyes on your mother!"

"Oh, I'm scared," he snickered. "Your sister's going to be dead unless she tells me where it is."

"With a whole government task force here? Sure, Tracy, go ahead," I said.

Bran's expression turned sour. "Will, you don't fight fair."

"I don't. And I don't care to. So let her go," I demanded.

"I put the thumb drive down the drain. I pulled out the stopper and just dropped it in," Tracy said quickly. "It's in the bathroom next to Bran's study in the main house."

"Oh, you fucking bitch!" He started shaking her.

"Miss Franz, I need you to have a good hold on the banister." Roseline's voice was calm.

Tracy locked her arms around two spindles.

Bran frowned down at Roseline. "And just what do you intend to d—?"

Roseline shot him in the shoulder.

He went stumbling backwards, shrieking.

"Miss Franz, I want you to come downstairs now," Roseline said.

Tracy let go of the railing and ran down the stairs. She launched herself into my arms.

I hugged her tightly.

"Calvin, Jim, arrest that man. We'll come up with a full list of charges on the way back to the facility." Roseline holstered her gun. "We'll probably add a whole lot more after we see what's on that thumb drive." She touched her earbud and told the others where to find the thumb drive.

"Can't I just kill him? Please?" I asked her while I held Tracy. "We can say it was self-defense."

"No. We're sending him to hell," Roseline replied. She touched her ear and nodded. "They found it. It's even dry, so probably no damage. But, just for fun, we're taking his electronics."

Tracy pulled away and wiped her eyes. "What happens now?"

"Well, I'm fairly certain your father is going to prison. Along with all those other men. But, on the plus side, you get to go home," Roseline said.

"They said they have some kind of failsafe that's going to blame me for all they've done," I told her. "McKenzie and Tracy will be implicated, too. As long as you keep McKenzie and Tracy out of this, I'm willing to go to prison."

"What?!" Tracy gasped. "No. No way. You're not going to prison! That's just crazy talk right there. You've worked so hard to get out. We all have. I mean, I kind of came on at the back end, but still!"

"Don't get too chivalrous yet. We're not complete idiots. I think the evidence will tell a different story." Roseline looked up as Calvin and Jim came down the stairs with Bran cuffed between them.

Bran scowled at her. "I need a doctor, bitch."

Roseline raised an eyebrow at him. "I'll think about it."

"I'm bleeding out!" he argued.

She looked at Jim.

"He's fine," Jim grunted.

"He's always been a big baby," I added.

Bran lunged at me but the two men held him back. "You sonofabitch. I hope you enjoy prison."

"I hope you do, too," I snarked.

"Take him away," Roseline said.

He was half-walked, half-dragged out of the guesthouse.

"I figure you want to go back to your estate to give your statements," Roseline assumed.

"Yes. We'd like that very much," I responded.

"Very much," Tracy agreed.

Roseline nodded and led the way out of the guesthouse and back to the Tahoe, just in time for us to see Bran being manhandled into a different SUV.

Another member of the task force ran up to Roseline with the thumb drive, grinning from ear to ear. "We've got it, ma'am."

"Excellent. Bag it and keep it separate from the rest of the evidence. I want something like nine techs to look at it the minute we get back to the facility. I have to make a stop to take statements." She speared the woman with a harsh look. "If any of that evidence disappears, I will put a boot so far up your ass you will be spitting shoe leather for the rest of your life, do you understand me? We are all tired of this bullshit!"

The woman swallowed. "Yes, ma'am."

We got in the Tahoe and started back to the Masterson Estate. Tracy looked far less shaken, which made me feel better. I was disappointed that I hadn't been able to kill Bran, but sending him to a third world prison hellscape was a close second.

"We are tired, ma'am," I said quietly. "This really has to be it. I don't think we can take much more of this—McKenzie's parents, especially. Her mom's about to crack up, and her dad's heart is...

well… I just don't think it can take the strain of much more happening. His body's pretty battered."

"I know." Roseline turned back to look at us from the passenger seat. "I'm sorry we've failed you so many times."

I shrugged. "You were up against people with a lot of money to throw around. It's frustrating, but understandable."

Her expression turned sympathetic. "From now on, everything is going to be okay."

"Don't make promises you can't keep." I sighed. "But thank you for the sentiment."

"This is one promise I intend to keep. I'm going to make sure you are all taken care of, if it takes me to my last breath. You're good people. You've worked hard to take down a ring of soulless assholes who don't deserve to breathe the same air that we do. And you've been betrayed over and over again. By people in my own agency, even. That ends today," she said.

I had the overwhelming urge to cry, but I swallowed it down. "Thank you, ma'am."

"Not going to call me Roseline anymore, boss?" she grinned.

"Is that even your real name?" I countered.

She laughed. "Touché."

"Then no, I think I won't." I shook my head. "You were a damn good executive assistant, though. Shame to lose you."

"You might see me around for a little while longer."

"Good," I smiled.

24

NOT BLINDED

McKenzie

It had been two weeks since our house was searched and Bran had been arrested. Two weeks, without a word.

A week ago, Rosaline disappeared from the office without notice. But we'd been sort of expecting that.

Will slept beside me, really sleeping now that we weren't on the run or being shot at or kidnapped or all the other crap that had been dominating our lives for over a year. I gently stroked his hair.

I was not sleeping well. I didn't think I would until everyone was arrested, there'd been a trial or seven, and we could finally put all this behind us.

At least Mom and Dad were doing well. Mom spent all the time she wasn't spending with Dad with Camille, who had quit the FBI to stay with us. The way she put it, she'd had a long and successful career and now it was time to do something else.

Dad was getting around under his own power. He still needed physical therapy, but he did that at home. He also spent a lot of time in the pool, working on getting back into shape.

Tracy decided to stay with us, which was great. Will and I didn't worry so much about her now that she was back under our roof.

Though, she'd probably be insulted that a twenty-year-old was fretting about a twenty-four-year-old.

I smiled at the thought.

Will mumbled something in his sleep, then snuggled close to me, draping an arm across my waist. "Honeybee," he snored.

It took everything in me not to burst out laughing.

There was a soft knock at the door. When Mom poked her head in, I put a finger to my lips.

She smiled and brought over a tray of waffles, bacon, and eggs, setting it on the bedside table. 'I love you,' she mouthed before tiptoeing back out.

I sighed happily and laid my head back down on the pillow. I wished it was all over.

"Still not sleeping?" Will yawned and kissed my cheek.

"No. I just have a bad feeling," I explained. "I feel really silly about it, but I just can't shake it."

"Don't feel silly. We've been through a lot. It's natural you would be bracing for the next thing," he said.

"That's true." I turned and put my arms around him. "I hate feeling this way."

He palmed my breast, gently playing with my nipple. "Want me to make you feel better for a little while?"

"Yeah," I whispered. "I do." I put my hand over his, helping him rub me just right.

Will groaned and kissed me. He rolled me underneath him, spreading my legs with his knee.

I was eager to dismiss my thoughts as soon as possible. I reached down and took his dick in my hand, beginning to stroke it.

"So unfair," he said as his cock swelled in my hand.

I thumbed a bead of precum off his tip and put it in my mouth, sucking pornographically while holding his gaze.

He shivered and slipped two fingers inside me.

I moaned.

"Wrap your legs around my waist," he said while he finger-fucked me.

Already panting, I did what he asked.

Another finger followed the first two. I knew, once he got his pinky in, I was going to get railed.

He worked me like it was his job—with real dedication.

I whimpered.

"That's it, honeybee. Give me more of that sweet honey," he murmured.

His pinky easily slid inside, and he ran his thumb over my clit.

"Oh God..." I moaned. "Oh God, oh—!"

I came around his fingers.

Will pulled his fingers out and, just as I'd done with his precum, sucked them clean while staring me in the eyes.

"Please..." I begged, my whole body shivering in the aftermath of my orgasm and in anticipation of my next. "Fuck me, Will."

He grinned. "My pleasure." He lined himself up and pushed deep inside me.

I arched my back, taking all of him.

"Such a greedy little honeypot," he smiled. "Fuck me, you feel so good."

"You, too," I replied, trying to catch my breath, only to lose it again when he started to thrust. I gripped his shoulders, digging my nails into his skin as he filled me over and over again.

Will groaned, and I could tell from the tension in his body that he was close. "Come for me, honeybee."

Two more thrusts and I ended up clawing his shoulders as I came, crying out his name.

He grunted and came hard inside me, pumping me full of his got cum.

"Holy fuck," he whispered, collapsing on top of me. "It just keeps getting better and better. If it keeps up like this, I'm going to have a heart attack by the time I'm forty!"

I smacked his arm. "Don't talk like that! Nobody's having a heart attack. Just rocking good sex."

"We're going to end up having so many kids," he mumbled, rolling tiredly to the side and taking me with him so he could stay buried inside me.

"Two. Max," I said. "And not until we're married, I'm done with school, and I've had time to build my career a little bit."

"Fair enough." He kissed my hair. "Three kids?"

"Two."

"I suppose two works as long as one of them is a little girl who looks just like you," he smiled.

"I was actually hoping for a little boy who looks just like you," I said. "But as long as they're both healthy…."

"Agreed." He stroked his fingertips up and down my spine. "Do you still want to go to the U? You can go anywhere now. Money's no object."

I gave that some thought. He was right. I didn't *have* to go to the University of Minnesota. Hell, I could probably go to Harvard if I wanted to.

But the more I thought about it, the more I decided against changing colleges. "I actually really like it there. And it's not six states away. It's a good school with a great reputation. And, I think I'd like to finish what I started. Maybe I'll go somewhere else for my masters, but only if you can come with me."

"I like that idea. I'll find someone to watch the business while I'm gone and we can have our own two-to-four-year adventure. Unless you want to be a doctor and then we'll just have a very long adventure," he said.

"I think I'll like adventuring with you. Just not as intense as the adventures we've already had," I replied.

"No. Not as intense as those." He nuzzled my neck. "How are you feeling about—?"

Someone banged insistently on our door.

Will quickly pulled out of me and yanked the covers up, and that was all the time we had before Camille burst through the door.

"You have to get out of here!" she said. "They're coming!"

My heart leapt into my throat. "Who's coming?!"

"The FBI! Katie—er—Roseline just called. They're following that stupid planted evidence and are planning to take you all to jail!" she cried. She went to the closet and began packing a bag for us.

There wasn't time to be modest about being naked. Will and I jumped out of bed.

Camille threw clothes at us and we got dressed.

"What about my parents? Tracy?" I asked, yanking on pants.

"I told Jacey. She's already grabbing Caleb and Tracy." She grabbed a second bag. "Is there cash in your office safe?" she asked Will.

"Yes. I'll go get it."

She tossed the empty bag to him.

He ran out of the room.

Together, Camille and I zipped the suitcase shut. I grabbed the handle. She hugged me.

"Good luck," she said.

I took a deep breath to stop my tears and darted out of the bedroom.

Mom and Dad were already assembled. Mom looked panicked. Dad had his arm around her.

"What's wrong?" I asked.

"Tracy went shopping. I texted her, but she won't be able to get back in time!" she choked. "We're going to have to leave her!"

"No!" I shook my head. "Maybe we can pick her up on our way—"

There was a slam against the front door.

"Open up! FBI!" a male voice barked.

"I just knew this wasn't over. I knew it! We should have run sooner!" I looked around, wondering where we could possibly go.

"Miss Trent."

I looked up and saw Dan, Garrett, and Eric standing at the back door.

"We've got the car running. We just need to go out the back gate," Garrett said calmly. He looked as though he'd been beaten up pretty badly, and Eric was also worse for the wear. But they were both still packing Glocks.

"They'll cover the back gate," Camille replied, coming up next to me. "We should have been faster!"

"We just need a distraction." Will came out of the office, holding the duffel bag. "I'm it."

"What?" I responded.

He handed Dad the bag. "There's a hundred-thousand dollars in there. Use it wisely."

"Will, you can't possibly—" Mom began.

"I have to. It's the only way." He looked at me, his eyes shimmering with unshed tears.

"No. *No!*" I beat on his chest as he pulled me into a hug. "No, I can't lose you!"

"You're not going to lose me. This is just a temporary misunderstanding. Once it's sorted out, we'll all come back home. And we'll get married. And you'll go to school. And we'll have three kids running around," he whispered into my hair.

I choked back a sob. "Two."

"We'll discuss the details later." He kissed me. "Now, go!"

I couldn't move, so he gave me a shove.

Mom took me by the wrist and dragged me out the back door.

There was another loud bang at the front door, only this time, the wood splintered.

Camille stood next to Will while Garrett, Eric, and Dan escorted us out.

We waited just out of sight at the back gate. When the gunfire started back inside the house, I wrenched free of Mom's grip and began running back in that direction.

Garrett scooped me and literally carried me, kicking and screaming, out the back gate.

The distraction worked. FBI agents came out of the woodwork, abandoning their posts near the vehicles and running toward the gate.

Eric, Garrett, and Dan, who, to my surprise, was also packing, shot them.

They fell to the ground, clutching shoulders and legs.

"Get in," Garrett said, opening the door for Mom and Dad. "And take her."

Dad grabbed me in a vice-like grip while Mom slammed my seatbelt into place.

Dan got behind the wheel while I struggled.

"Will!" I yelled. "Will!"

Garrett got in the front seat next to Dan, while Eric took the very back row of the Escalade for himself.

We peeled around the side of the house.

I saw a stretcher being wheeled out onto the street, the face covered by a white sheet.

"Oh God, no…" I gasped. "Will…."

Much to my relief, however, Will was marched out right afterward, his hands behind his head. They roughly forced him to kneel on the ground.

Then, before anyone could react, we zoomed past the FBI and away from the Masterson Estate.

It was the last I saw of Will for a very, very long time.

2 5

NOWHERE TO GO

Tracy

Not knowing what else to do, I went home to my father. I was still holding a rather large shopping haul because it never occurred to me to leave it behind. I was running completely on autopilot.

I walked into the house, only to see the place had been completely turned upside down. "Dad?" I called, dropping my bags in the hall. "What's going on?"

"I'm leaving," he said, coming out of his office. "You should think about it, too."

"Why are *you* leaving?" I asked. "You're not implicated."

"It's just a matter of time before they see through the bullshit. They might be government, but even they aren't stupid." He was rolling a large, locked case behind him.

"Where are we going?" I looked at the case. "Is that money?"

"You bet your ass that's money. And *we* aren't going anywhere. You're on your own, kid. I'm not going to let you betray me again." He sneered at me.

I folded my arms over my chest. "Well, if you weren't a sex-trafficking bastard, we wouldn't be having this conversation."

"Your opinion doesn't matter to me, Tracy. It never did. All you

187

had to do was look pretty and catch a rich man. Preferably one I could do business with. Now? You are absolutely useless to me. Damaged goods," he said.

"Love you, too," I snapped. I tried to pretend his words didn't hurt me, but it was hard.

He snorted. "Like love ever had anything to do with it. Useless cow."

I slapped him. My fingernails drew blood.

My father touched his cheek, then gave me a mirthless grin. "Go spread your legs for someone who can help you. I'm out." He shoved me aside and headed for the door. "Oh, and there's no more money. Not any. So I'd be careful using your credit card."

"I don't want your blood money!" I yelled after him.

"Too bad. Because you're going to need it." He left, slamming the door behind him.

I stared after him in shock. His words cut deep.

He'd never loved me at all?

It made sense, in a heartbreaking way.

I sank down on the sofa for all of thirty seconds, then realized I couldn't stay. The FBI would be coming. I grabbed my purse and headed to the garage.

Because it was what I usually drove, I rejected the cute little BMW convertible and went instead for the sedan our chauffeur drove us around in. He seemed surprised to see me, and doubly surprised to see me taking the keys for the town car.

"Miss Franz?" Stephen asked.

"I've got to get out of here, Steve. I'll bring it back if I can. Otherwise, the cops will impound it, and you can pick it up there. Also, Mr. Franz drained all the accounts, as far as I can tell. I don't think he'll be paying any of the staff this month," I informed him.

Stephen nodded. "Thank you for telling me."

"Oh, and when the FBI gets here, let them do whatever they want. Just don't send them after me," I said.

"Can do, Miss Franz. Good luck."

That he didn't question the situation at all told me volumes about what he must have overheard in the car over the years.

I slid into the town car and drove out of the garage, rounding a corner outside the gate just as police cars with flashing lights showed up well behind me.

It pained me to do something this illegal—I was against cell phones and driving—but I had little choice in the matter. While I navigated the streets around Lake Minnetonka, I carefully punched in my mother's number.

She didn't answer.

I tried again.

No answer.

I sighed. This was not unusual for my mother. It was half the reason I'd gone no contact with her. But I couldn't exactly be choosy about where I could get help now.

The sixth time I called her, my mother answered with a loud huff. "What do you need, Tracy?"

"I'm in trouble," I said without preamble. "Dad did some very bad things, and now I'm implicated. I don't know what to do or where to go. I need help!"

I could feel her rolling her eyes on the other end of the line. "Tracy, honestly, you're so stupid. How did you manage to get implicated in Morgan's schemes?"

My blood went cold. "You knew?"

"Of course I knew! But I wasn't dumb enough to get myself tangled up in it," she sniffed.

"How could you know and not report him?! Did you really know what he was doing?!" I gaped.

"Don't be so dramatic. He wasn't doing anything that other people haven't been doing since the dawn of time. It paid for our lifestyle. I certainly wasn't giving that up," she scoffed.

I couldn't believe what I was hearing. "Fine. Why didn't you report him when you left him for the count?"

"A nondisclosure agreement. I wasn't giving up that kind of money just so that some starving kid in Africa could die in poverty, rather than grow up eating three meals a day. All they have to do is a little cleaning."

My jaw dropped. "You're a monster."

"And you're just like Nate. No sense of reality. Just all puffed up on virtue. God, I can't believe I was married to that man. He was so insufferable." My mother sighed theatrically.

"I can't believe I'm still asking this, but will you help me?" I asked, feeling icky.

"Hm. Vlad doesn't really like children…" she mused.

"I'm twenty-four!" I argued.

She paused. "Exactly! I don't need that kind of competition. Next thing you know, Vlad will run off with you before I have the next one lined up!"

"Oh my God, you are not serious right now!" I wished I could reach through the phone and shake her.

"I am. Don't contact me again. I was rather liking our little stand-off. I don't see why we ever need to speak in the future." She hung up on me.

The phone slipped from my fingers. *Who's going to help me now?!*

Then, I remembered what my mother said about Nate.

Nate was, if I was counting correctly, her fourth husband. I was sixteen when they married. I was at the wedding, even stood in as the dutiful junior bridesmaid in the bridal party for my mother. I could tell he loved my mother, and I felt sorry for the guy because I knew she was going to dump him as soon as she found someone richer or more famous. But especially richer.

My mother's other husbands had been jaded enough to know the deal. But Nate? Not so much. I was sure he was plenty jaded now, however. After my mother dropped him like a hot potato for Alan Alejandro, a famous Spanish actor who came from a rich family, I knew he'd been crushed.

I hadn't seen a lot of him. By the time I was twelve, my mother decided she wanted little to nothing to do with raising a child, and so gave up full custody to my father.

But I knew he adored her. And she'd ripped his heart out and stomped on it.

Still, as my mother said, of all her husbands, he was the one who was truly honest. And good. An actual good man.

Without thinking too much about it—because this was an insane plan—I turned my car in the direction of the Twin Cities.

I got to Alton Tower in the late afternoon. The sun was setting, and it was chilly outside. I hadn't brought a jacket, but I didn't care. I stopped at the valet station, got out, and handed them my keys.

Taking a deep breath, I walked into the building. "This is insane," I muttered to myself as I went to the security desk. "This is absolutely insane."

The two guards at the desk looked up as I approached. "Can I help you?" the woman asked.

I cleared my throat. Twice. "Yes. I would like to see Nathaniel Alton."

They stared at me. "Pardon?" she asked.

"Do you… have an appointment?" the man chimed in.

"No. I don't. But I think he'll see me. At least, I hope he will." I straightened my shoulders, drawing on the poise I'd learned in finishing school. "Please tell him Tracy Franz is here. Um… Lillian's daughter."

They looked at each other. "Well, Miss Franz, we can try…."

"Thank you. That's all I ask."

The woman nodded in the direction of a few chairs gathered around a coffee table. "We'll come get you when we hear back from him."

"Oh. Thank you." I wandered over to the chairs and sat down heavily. I couldn't help it. I dropped my head in my hands. "Fuck," I whispered to myself.

Twenty minutes passed. Then an hour. Then two. I glanced several times at the desk, but the two of them wouldn't even look at me.

They hadn't sent me away, though, so that gave me a modicum of hope.

The sun set, but I just kept staring at my clasped hands in my lap. "This is completely insane. I should leave."

But I had nowhere to go.

Security had a shift change and now there were two men at the desk. Before leaving, the woman had pointed at me and said something to them.

They'd nodded and started ignoring me as well.

I checked my phone. Nine PM.

I hoped McKenzie, Will, and the others were okay.

Finally, at ten-thirty, the desk phone rang. One of the men answered it and looked up at me. "Yes, sir. Right away." He hung up and walked over.

"Mr. Alton will see you now," he said stiffly. "I'll show you up."

"Thank you," I said, standing. My legs felt like jelly, and I really had to pee. But I hadn't wanted to miss my opportunity. "Can we stop by the restroom first?"

"No. Mr. Alton will not be kept waiting," he replied.

Great. Pissing my pants it is. I just nodded and followed him to the elevator.

He pressed a button for the fortieth floor and tapped his ID badge to a sensor.

There was no going back now.

The guard walked me straight through the empty executive floor. The lights were off except for the emergency overheads. Everyone had gone home for the evening.

We stopped before large, dark wood double doors.

The guard knocked.

"Come in," Nate called from the other side. I still recognized his voice.

The guard opened the door and gave me a little push on the back when I didn't immediately walk through.

Nate was sitting behind his desk, his fingers steepled in front of him. "Miss Franz."

He sounded cold.

The door closed behind me.

Shit.

"Mr. Alton," I replied, since we were being formal. "Thank you for seeing me."

"It didn't seem as though you were getting the point of my snub, so I decided it must be something truly urgent. Is Lillian dead?" he asked conversationally.

"No. She's… fine." I settled on the word 'fine.' It wouldn't do to air the family's dirty laundry all at once.

"Pity."

I winced. Sure, she was a flaming bitch, but she was still my mother.

He tapped his chin. "Hm."

As he regarded me, I took the opportunity to look at him. He still had the same brown hair, though there were silver strands peeking through it. He was built beneath his suit, more than he had been when he was with my mother. And his warm brown eyes… were no longer warm.

That gave me a chill, but also made me sad for some reason.

"All right. I'll bite. What brings you here, Miss Franz?" he asked.

This was the worst mistake of my life. I looked back at the door. "I…."

I should leave.

"I…."

There's nowhere to go.

I swallowed. Nate was my only hope. "Mr. Alton, I'm in trouble."

ALSO BY M. FRANCIS HASTINGS

Once Bitten

Submitting to My Stepbrother series

Stranded With My Stepbrother

Snatched With My Stepbrother

Sequestered With My Stepbrother

Subpoenaed With My Stepbrother

Flirting With the Forbidden

Fleeing With the Forbidden

Fighting for the Forbidden

Forever With the Forbidden

The Beguiling Baronets series

Deceiving the Duke

Dream Mates

Dream Weaver

Dream Reader